Lara Vapnyar

# Broccoli and Other
# Tales of Food and Love

Lara Vapnyar emigrated from Russia in 1994. She is
also the author of the novel *Memoirs of a Muse*, and a
story collection, *There Are Jews in My House*, which
was nominated for the Los Angeles Times Book Prize
and the New York Public Library Young Lions Fiction Award, and won the Prize for Jewish Fiction by
Emerging Writers from the National Foundation for
Jewish Culture. Her work has appeared in *The New
York Times*, *The New Yorker*, and *Open City*. She lives
with her family on Staten Island.

ALSO BY LARA VAPNYAR

*Memoirs of a Muse*

*There Are Jews in My House*

# BROCCOLI AND OTHER TALES OF FOOD AND LOVE

# BROCCOLI
## AND
## OTHER TALES
### OF
## FOOD AND LOVE

STORIES

Lara Vapnyar

Anchor Books
A Division of Random House, Inc.
New York

FIRST ANCHOR BOOKS EDITION, JUNE 2009

*Copyright © 2008 by Lara Vapnyar*

All rights reserved. Published in the United States by Anchor Books, a division
of Random House, Inc., New York, and in Canada by Random House of Canada
Limited, Toronto. Originally published in hardcover in the United States by
Pantheon Books, a division of Random House, Inc., New York, in 2008.

Anchor Books and colophon are registered trademarks of Random House, Inc.

Some of the stories in this collection originally appeared in the following:
"Borscht" in *Harper's*; "A Bunch of Broccoli on the Third Shelf" and
"Luda and Milena" in *The New Yorker*; and "Puffed Rice and Meatballs" in
*Zoetrope: All-Story*. "Puffed Rice and Meatballs" also appeared in
*O. Henry Prize Stories 2006*, edited by Laura Furman (Anchor Books,
a division of Random House, Inc., New York, 2006).

The Library of Congress has cataloged the Pantheon edition as follows:
Vapnyar, Lara.
Broccoli and other tales of food and love / Lara Vapnyar.
p. cm.
1. Russians—United States—Fiction. 2. Immigration—Fiction. I. Title.
PS3622.A68B76  2008
813'.6—dc22  2007041537

Anchor ISBN: 978-0-307-27988-0

*Book design by Robert C. Olsson*

www.anchorbooks.com

# CONTENTS

# BROCCOLI AND OTHER TALES OF FOOD AND LOVE

# *A Bunch of Broccoli on the Third Shelf*

*A*NOTHER ONE, seduced and abandoned," Nina's husband said, pulling a bunch of wilted broccoli from the refrigerator shelf. He held it with two fingers as if it stank, his handsome face scrunched in a grimace of disgust.

It doesn't stink, Nina thought. She blushed and hurried to take the broccoli—to throw it into the garbage. It isn't fresh, but you can't say that it stinks. She didn't say these thoughts aloud. She said she was sorry, she was busy all week and didn't have time for cooking. Nina worked in Manhattan. By the time she came home to Brooklyn, it was already seven thirty, sometimes eight, and she felt too tired to cook. The most she could do was fix a sandwich for her husband and herself or boil some meat dumplings from a Russian food store.

"Yes, I know," her husband said. "But why buy all these vegetables if you know you won't have time to cook them?" Nina shrugged. She liked shopping for vegetables.

Nina couldn't say when she'd first begun the habit of shopping for vegetables. Probably two years earlier, on her second day in America, when she and her husband left her sister's Brooklyn apartment to explore the nearest shopping street. Her sister, who'd lived in America for fourteen years, called herself an American. She thought Nina would be impatient to see everything. "Go, go," her sister said. "But don't buy anything. To survive in America, there are two rules you have to remember. First: Never buy anything in expensive stores unless they have a fifty-percent-off sale. Second: Never *ever* buy anything in cheap stores."

On the street with the unimaginative name *Avenue M*, they walked through narrow stores that all looked alike to Nina, no matter what they sold: food, electronics, clothes, or hardware. After a while, it seemed that they were walking in and out of the same store over and over, just to hear the chime of its bell. The February morning was cold, and the sunlight was pale. Nina hid her reddened nose in the fur collar of her Russian coat. She clutched her husband's elbow and carefully stepped over piles of garbage, reluctant to look up or sideways at the ashen sky or the motley signs of the shops. She felt dizzy and a little nauseated from the flight and the all-night talk with her sister. Only one place attracted her attention: a small Korean grocery with fruits and vegetables set outside on plywood stands—colorful piles of oranges, tomatoes, and cucumbers, almost unnaturally clean and bright. Nina read the sign on the box of tomatoes: SUNRIPE. She was still learning English, and every new expression seemed exciting and full of great meaning. SUNRIPE brought to mind a vegetable patch on a summer afternoon, the smell of the rich soil heated by the sun, palegreen branches sagging under heavy tomatoes bursting with juice. SUNRIPE reminded her of her family's tiny vegetable garden when she was little. Nina wanted to touch the tomatoes in the box, hoping that their surface would still be a little warm from all the sun that shined on them while they ripened. She was reaching for one when her husband dragged her away to another store.

Now Nina shopped alone for vegetables every Saturday morning while her husband slept late. Nina drove to 86th Street to visit the Korean and Russian vegetables stores between 22nd and 23rd avenues. The assortment in the stores was generally the same, but Nina liked to explore each of them, hoping to find something surprising, such as the occasional white asparagus, or plastic baskets of gooseberries, or tiny nutlike new potatoes.

On days when there weren't any new or exciting items, it was still interesting to compare the stores. In one store the onions could be large and shiny, but the bunches of lettuce wilted and colorless. Another store could boast of the freshest, brightest lettuce, while the squashy gray onions hid timidly in string bags.

Nina felt a thrill as soon as she climbed out of the car by a store entrance, her feet touching a sidewalk littered with bits of lettuce, onion peel, and broken tomatoes. Inside, she walked between the produce shelves, touching the fruit and vegetables and marveling at how different their surfaces felt. She ran her fingers over the tomatoes; they felt smooth and glossy like polished furniture. She cupped oranges, feeling their lumpy skins in her palms. Sometimes she would hook an orange peel with her nail so it would sputter a little of its pungent, spicy juice on her finger. She avoided the hairy egg-shaped kiwis and wormlike string beans. She liked to stroke the light, feathery bunches of dill and parsley, and to squeeze artichokes, which felt like pine cones, but soft ones. She liked to pat cantaloupes and tap watermelons with her index finger to hear the hollow sound they made. Most of all, Nina loved broccoli. It smelled of young spring grass, and it looked like a spring tree with its solid stem and luxuriant crown of tight grainy florets that resembled recently blossomed leaves.

Regardless of the other vegetables she bought, Nina took home a bunch of broccoli every week. She carried the heavy brown bags proudly to the car with the firm belief that this weekend she would find time to cook. There was the rest of Saturday afternoon ahead, and all of Sunday. She would wash the vegetables as soon as she got home and then cook something on Sunday, maybe spinach gnocchi, or grilled zucchini, or broccoli topped with a three-cheese sauce.

Somehow, Nina invariably managed to forget both the errands she had to run on Sundays and the Saturday-night parties at her husband's friend's. As soon as she came home, Nina immediately found herself in a whirl of things to do. She had to shower in a hurry, hot-curl her hair, brush it down if it turned out too frizzy, try on and reject various sweaters and pants, put on her makeup, find her husband's socks, iron his shirt, tell him where his other sock was, check if the gas was off, and lock the door.

In what seemed like only a minute, Nina found herself back in the car on the way to the party. She alternately glanced at her husband in the driver's seat and at her reflection in the mirror. Her husband seemed distant and deep in his thoughts, which was natural, she told herself, because he was driving. And her own reflection seemed unsatisfying. Her hair was still too frizzy, her soft-featured round face required a different type of makeup, and her blue angora pullover cut into her armpits. The thing about clothes bought at fifty-percent-off sales was that they were either the wrong size or the wrong design. In the car, Nina didn't think about vegetables. They lay abandoned on the refrigerator shelves, where Nina had shoved them in a hurry: tomatoes squashed under zucchini, lettuce leaves jammed against the edge of the vegetable basket, a bunch of broccoli that didn't fit anywhere else placed all by itself on the third shelf.

The parties were held at Pavlik's place, Nina's husband's friend from work, whose wife had divorced him a few years earlier. Pavlik was a heavy man with an uneven ginger-colored beard. He wore ill-fitting trousers and unclean shirts. He loved to laugh heartily and smack his friends on the back. "Don't mind the mess!" he yelled, as his guests wandered through the dusty labyrinth of his house, stumbling on mismatched furniture, broken electronic equipment, heavy volumes of Russian books, and slippery magazines. It seemed to Nina that Pavlik's function as a host was limited to yelling, "Don't mind the mess!" He didn't feed or entertain his guests. People came to him with their own food and wine, their own plastic dinnerware, their own guitars, and sometimes their own poems written in notebooks.

Not one of Pavlik's guests was a professional poet or musician, though. Most of them worked as computer programmers, the occupation they took up in America, finding it easier and more profitable than trying to prove the value of their Russian degrees in science or the arts. Some of them, Nina's husband included, adopted a condescending, slightly snobbish attitude to their new profession, as something easy and boring, something beneath them. "A computer programmer, like everybody else," they answered reluctantly, when asked about their present profession. "But that's not what I used to be in my previous life." They preferred to talk about art or music or their exciting hobbies, such as mountain climbing, rafting, or photographing Alaskan sunsets.

Nina was a computer programmer too, but unlike everybody else she'd also been a computer programmer in her "previous life." What was worse, she didn't know much about poetry or music, and she didn't have any exciting talents or hobbies.

"My wife is a vegetable lover," Nina's husband said, introducing her to Pavlik's circle.

Nina didn't like Pavlik's guests. The men were untidy and unattractive. They piled up their paper plates with cold cuts, smoked too much, and laughed with their mouths full. They repeated the same things over and over, and it seemed to Nina that there was always a piece of ham or salami hanging from their mouths while they talked.

The women, on the other hand, with the exception of one or two, were attractive but in a wrong, unpleasant way. They were thin and sophisticated, with straight hair and strong hands with long powerful fingers, toughened by playing either the piano or the guitar. They had soulful eyes, sad from all the poetry they read, and wore expressions of eternal fatigue. They had everything that Nina lacked.

Nina usually sat through the whole evening in the corner of Pavlik's stiff sofa, away from the other guests, who sat on the floor by the cold fireplace, and away from her husband. The sounds of their laughter, their singing, and their reading floated around the room but didn't seem to reach her. The food and wine on a rickety folding table by the window were more accessible from the sofa. Nina made frequent trips to that table, where cold cuts lay on paper plates, loaves of bread stood on cutting boards, and pickles swam in glass jars with a fork invariably stuck into one of them. There were usually a few unopened bottles of vodka, and a five-liter box of Burgundy or Chablis. The wine often dripped from the plastic spigot right onto the beige carpet, making intricate patterns, so that by the end of the party Pavlik's modest carpet looked like a fancy Turkish rug.

When they first started going to Pavlik's parties, Nina sat by the fireplace with the others. She loved to sit across from her husband and watch his face while he played. His neck was bent down, the bangs of his dark hair fallen over his half-closed eyes. From time to time he glanced at her, and then his eyes flickered through the forest of his hair like two tiny lightning bugs. At those moments Nina felt he was playing for her, and then the music touched her, making her skin prickle and her throat hurt.

With time, Nina noticed that she wasn't the only one staring at her husband while he played. Nina saw how the faces of other women lit up just like hers under his fleeting gaze. Each of them must have felt that he was playing for her. Sometimes Nina thought those women had more right to be looked at by her husband. Sometimes those women threw quick looks at Nina, and then Nina felt that she was changing in size; she was growing, bloating up, turning into an enormous exhibit: a dull, untalented woman wearing the wrong clothes and the wrong makeup. She thought that all of them must have wondered why this interesting, talented man had married her.

Her sister didn't wonder. "You were his ticket to America," she often reminded Nina, having first said it on Nina's arrival in New York. "Can you disprove that?"

Nina couldn't.

It was true that Nina's husband had always wanted to emigrate but couldn't obtain a visa. He didn't have close relatives in the United States. It was true that, having married Nina, he had gotten his visa. And it was true that Nina hadn't wanted to emigrate but yielded to her husband's wishes. But it wasn't true that he had married Nina just for that, and it wasn't true that he didn't love her. Nina's sister didn't know what Nina knew. She didn't know that when Nina was in the hospital after appendix surgery, her husband wouldn't leave her room even for a minute. She begged him to go and have some coffee or to take a breath of fresh air, but he refused. He held Nina's hand and squeezed it every time she moaned. Nina's sister didn't know how sometimes he would hug Nina from behind, bury his face in her hair, and whisper, "There is nothing like it. Nothing in the world." She could feel his sharp nose and his hot breath on the nape of her neck, and her eyes would grow moist. And Nina's sister didn't know that he often said the same words when they were making love.

It was a relief to come home after the party

and find herself in bed, next to her husband, with a book. Nina had covered the nightstand with cookbooks bought at a fifty-percent discount at Barnes & Noble. She read lying on her back, using her stomach to prop up her book. The thick, glossy pages rustled against Nina's satin night-gowns (fifty-percent off at Victoria's Secret). She loved the rustling sound as much as she loved the prickly sensation in her feet when they touched her husband's hairy legs from time to time. She also loved the euphoric feeling roused in her by lustrous photographs of okra and tomato stew in rustic clay bowls, grilled zucchini parcels on ceramic trays, and baskets of fresh vegetables against a background of meadows or olive groves. Her favorite book, *Italian Cuisine: The Taste of the Sun,* included step-by-step photographs of the cooking process. In the photos, smooth light-skinned female hands with evenly trimmed fingernails performed all the magical actions on the vegetables. They looked like Nina's hands, and Nina fantasized that they were hers. It was she, Nina, who made those perfect curled carrot slices. It was she who pushed the hard, stubborn stuffing into the bell peppers, or rinsed grit off lettuce leaves, or chopped broccoli florets, scattering tiny green crumbs all over the table. Nina's lips moved, forming the rich, passionate words of the cooking instructions: "Brush with olive oil," "bring to a boil and simmer gently," "serve hot," "scoop out the pulp," "chop," "slice," "crush," "squash." When eventually she put the book away, cuddled against her husband's back, and closed her eyes, her lips continued moving for some time.

NINA'S HUSBAND left her during the middle of September, when the vegetable stores on 86th Street were full of tomatoes and zucchinis. There was an abundance of them in Nina's refrigerator when her sister opened it.

"The fifth week is the worst. The first four weeks it hasn't sunk in yet. You feel the shock, but you don't feel the pain. It's like you're numb. But the fifth week. . . . Brace yourself for the fifth week." Nina's sister crouched in front of the refrigerator, unloading the food she had brought. She came to console Nina with four large bags from a Russian food store.

Nina felt tired. She sat at the table, staring at her sister's broad back. Nina thought that if you tried to hit it with a hammer it would produce a loud ringing sound, as if her sister's back were made of hardwood. The refrigerator shelves filled quickly: bright cartons of currant juice— "Currant juice saved my life; I basically lived on it when Volodya left me"—cream cheese, farmer's cheese, soft cheese, Swiss cheese, bread—"Always keep bread in the refrigerator, it preserves much better this way"—pickles, a jar of cherry compote.

"Nina!" her sister suddenly shrieked. "What is this?" She pulled out a vegetable basket. Inside was a pile of mushy tomatoes with a white beard of mold where the skin split, oozing dark juice; zucchini covered with brown splotches; dark, slimy bunches of collard greens. "You've got the whole vegetable graveyard in here." Her sister emptied the basket into the garbage can, where the vegetables made a squashing sound.

The faint rotten smell stayed in the kitchen for a long time after Nina's sister left. The smell wasn't unpleasant. It was a simple, cozy kitchen smell, like vegetable soup simmering on the stove, the kind Nina's mother used to make.

Contrary to her sister's prediction, the fifth week didn't bring Nina any extreme pain but only added to her fatigue. Nina felt as if she were recovering from a long, exhausting illness. She tried to do as few household chores as possible. She didn't shop for vegetables anymore. She still read her cookbooks after work, but she was too tired to decipher the recipes. Instead, she ran her finger over the index pages, which were filled with neat columns of letters. The austere phrases were logical and easy to read: "Broccoli: gratin, 17; macaroni with, 71; penne and, 79." She had no desire to look up the recipe on the referred page, she simply went on to the next entry that caught her eye: "Eggplant: braised chicken with orange and, 137."

Pavlik's booming voice on the old, creaky answering machine broke into the elegant sequence of string bean recipes. Nina had turned off the ringer on the phone weeks earlier and now only listened to messages as they came through her machine. Most often they were from Nina's sister, who called to ask if Nina was eating well and to tell her the latest news: that Nina's husband had been seen on Brighton Beach with some "dried herring," then that he was moving to Boston, then that he had already moved. Her sister's voice seemed to Nina distant and somewhat unnatural.

Pavlik's voice made her jump. "Hey! Nina! Are you home?" he shouted.

On impulse, Nina looked at the front door. It was hard to believe that all that roaring came from a modest plastic box on the kitchen counter. Pavlik's voice suddenly went low, and it became hard to make out his words. "Don't disappear," he said, if Nina heard him correctly.

PAVLIK'S PLACE looked different. Nina saw it as soon as she stepped into his living room, but she couldn't quite figure out why. The rickety food table still stood on the "Turkish" rug, the fireplace was crammed with piles of old magazines, Pavlik's hulking figure was shaking with laughter, and the vacant sofa was waiting for Nina in the corner. Everything was there, everything was in the same place, yet something was undeniably different. The size—it's become bigger, Nina decided, taking her seat between the sofa cushions. Pavlik's place had more space and more air.

A thin, delicate woman's voice sang something about a little path in the woods that meandered among the trees. Just like the words in this song, Nina thought. She liked the song. When it ended, the singer put her guitar down and walked to the food table. She was wearing a long gray cardigan with drooping pockets. There wasn't anything mysterious about her. A balding man with a closely trimmed gray beard took over the guitar. Nina's eyes traveled from the man's outstretched elbow protruding through his shabby corduroy sleeve, to his stooped shoulder, to the greasy line of his hair. Nina suddenly saw that his untidiness wasn't some kind of snobbish fashion statement but a sign of loneliness, of being uncared for. She saw that the women sitting in a circle were watching the man just as they used to watch her husband. They were tired, lonely women, just as she was. There wasn't anything mysterious about them either. Nina also noticed that she wasn't the only one sitting outside the singing circle. In fact, only a few people sat in the circle, while others were scattered all around Pavlik's house. A lonely figure here and there sat quietly on a chair, an old box, or a windowsill, or wandered around the room. From time to time the paths of the lonely figures intersected, and then conversations were struck: awkward yet hopeful conversations, just as the one Nina was having now.

"You are a vegetable lover, aren't you?" a man asked, having seated himself in the opposite corner of Nina's sofa.

Nina nodded.

"Yes, I thought I heard that from somebody. Do you like to cook vegetables?"

Nina nodded again.

"You know, I love vegetables myself. My wife hates it when I cook, though." The man rolled his eyes, making Nina smile. He was short, with thin rusty-red hair and a very pale complexion. A tiny piece of toilet paper with a spot of dried blood stuck to his cheek.

"Are you a computer programmer like everybody else?" Nina asked.

The man nodded with a smile.

"And in your previous life?"

"A physics teacher in high school. But I can't say that I miss it. I was terrified of my students."

Nina laughed. It was easy to talk to him. Nina

looked at his smiling eyes, then down at his hands—short fingernails, white fingers, red hair on the knuckles. She tried to imagine what it would be like if a hand like this brushed against her breast. Accidentally.

Nina wiped the little beads of sweat off her nose. He was a strange, married, and not particularly attractive man. He introduced himself as Andrei.

"So, what's your favorite vegetable?" Nina asked.

"I would say fennel. Fennel has an incredible flavor. Reminds me of a wild apple and, oddly enough, freshly sawed wood. Do you like fennel?"

Nina nodded. She liked fennel. It had a funny, slightly ribbed surface, and it was heavy and spouted weird green shoots that seemed to grow out of nowhere. Nina'd never tasted fennel. "I like broccoli," she said.

"Oh, broccoli! I love how they cook it in Chinese places. How do you cook it?"

This man with the piece of tissue stuck to his cheek looked safe enough to confide in. "I've never cooked broccoli—or any other vegetable," Nina said.

"Let's have a cooking date," Andrei offered.

A cooking date! Nina couldn't remember ever feeling so excited. She was sure she had been as excited sometime before, she just couldn't remember when. So the better part of the following Saturday Nina spent shopping for cooking utensils. She went to Macy's and abandoned the fifty-percent-discount rule for the first time, buying two drastically overpriced skillets, a set of shiny stainless steel saucepans, a steamer, and a pretty wooden spoon with a carved handle.

"Do you want it wrapped as a wedding present?" the cashier asked.

Halfway home, Nina realized that she hadn't bought nearly enough. Knives! She needed knives! And a cutting board, and a colander, and God knows what else. She swerved her car in the direction of Avenue M, where, abandoning the second rule about never ever buying anything in cheap stores, she bought a set of knives, two wooden cutting boards and one plastic, a colander, a curved grapefruit knife just because it looked so cute, a vegetable peeler, a set of stainless steel bowls, and two aprons with a picture of wild mushrooms on a yellow background. In a grocery store next door Nina bought a bottle of olive oil, black pepper, chili pepper, and a jar of something dry and dark-green with Chinese letters on it.

Well before three o'clock—the time of their cooking date—Nina had everything ready. The sparkling saucepans and the skillet stood proudly on the stove. The bowls, the colander, the cutting boards, and the knives were arranged on the kitchen counter in careful disarray around the centerpiece: the opened *Italian Cuisine: The Taste of the Sun.* Nina observed her kitchen, trying to shake off the embarrassing excess of excitement.

Andrei came on time, even earlier. At five minutes to three he already stood in Nina's hall, removing his bulky leather jacket and his leather cap sprinkled with raindrops. He smelled of wet leather. He handed Nina a bottle of wine and a baguette in a sodden paper bag. "In movies, when a man hands a woman a baguette and a bottle of wine, it always seems chic, doesn't it?" he said.

Nina nodded. Andrei looked more homely than she remembered. Nina's memory somehow had managed to erase the red spots on his pasty cheeks, to color his brows and eyelashes, to make him slimmer, and add an inch or two to his height. It was strange seeing him in her house, especially in her tiny hall, where every object was familiar, its place carefully considered. He clashed with the surroundings like a bad piece of furniture. Nina hurried to lead him into the kitchen.

"So, are we cooking broccoli today?" Andrei asked. He began leafing through *Italian Cuisine: The Taste of the Sun,* his freshly washed hands still smelling of Nina's soap.

"Broccoli, yes," Nina mumbled. She was suddenly struck by a dreadful suspicion, which was immediately confirmed upon opening the refrigerator.

In all her shopping frenzy, she had forgotten to buy any vegetables.

She jerked out the vegetable basket, faintly hoping for a miracle. The basket was empty and sparklingly clean, wiped with a kitchen towel moistened in Clorox by her sister's firm hand. There was only a tiny strip of onion skin stuck between the edge of the basket and the shelf above. Nina turned to Andrei, motioning to the empty basket. Her throat felt as if someone were squeezing it. Suddenly everything seemed hopeless and absurd: the counter crammed with gleaming, artificial sets of kitchenware; the barren vegetable basket; this perfect stranger, who came to cook in her kitchen; Nina herself, with all her energy and excitement of moments ago, now pressing her forehead against the cold vinyl of the refrigerator door.

"Do you want me to drive to a supermarket?" Andrei asked.

Nina shook her head. She knew it would never work now, after everything had been exposed to her in all its absurdity.

"What's this?" Andrei asked. He was looking toward the back of the refrigerator. A bunch of broccoli was stuck between the third shelf and the refrigerator wall. It hung upside down, the florets nearly touching the shelf below. The bunch wasn't yellowed or covered with rotten slime. On the contrary, for the weeks that it lay between the shelves, it had become darker and dryer. A few more weeks and it would have turned into a broccoli mummy. It smelled okay, or rather it didn't smell at all. "I'm sure we can still cook it," Andrei said. He began showing Nina what to do.

Nina ran cold water over the florets, then shook the bunch fiercely, letting out a shower of green drops. She chopped off the stem, then cut off the base of each floret, watching with fascination how they split into new tiny bunches of broccoli. She then peeled the stem and cut it into even, star-shaped slices. Some things turned out to be different from Nina's cooking fantasies, others exactly the same. Some were disappointing, others better than she ever imagined. The best thing of all was that, when the broccoli was already on the stove, sputtering boiling water from under the shiny lid, Andrei pulled one of her kitchen chairs close to the stove and suggested she stand on it.

"Climb up and inhale," he said. "The hot air travels up. The strongest aroma should be right under the ceiling." He stood back, giving her room.

Nina stood on the chair, her hair just grazing the ceiling. She closed her eyes, lifted her nose, and breathed in deep. The warm aroma of broccoli rose up, caressing Nina's face, enveloping the whole of her.

# *Borscht*

$S$ERGEY WOKE UP with an erection and a headache. The first was soon gone but the second lingered, radiating jagged rings of pain from a point of distress somewhere in the center of his skull.

He closed his eyes, hoping for the comfort of darkness, but saw instead the great hairy surface of the carpet that he had installed in New Jersey the day before. Sergey had been installing carpets for eight months, ever since Pavel had taken him on to work with him, and now whenever he closed his eyes he would see, smell, and even feel carpets. Yesterday's color was called Georgia Peach but was in fact a pale brown with a pinkish hue, bland and dry. The carpet smelled like dust, glistened with synthetic threads, and was dead to the touch.

All carpets were named after something bright and tempting. When Sergey began the job, he would often ask Pavel, who spoke good English, what this or that expression meant. "Warm honey," Pavel would translate, "Hawaiian waterfall," "Mulberry tree." The earthy tones were the most popular, and the same grayish-beige color could be called *Morning fog, Bay fog, Autumn leaves, Brown sugar,* or *Elk's horn.* At first, as Sergey measured, cut, and tucked, he would entertain himself by making up new, truer names for the carpet colors: *Moldy bread, Puddle of dirty water, Pig's feet, Cow dung on a warm day.* He had stopped doing this sometime ago. The names for the colors became just words for Sergey, simple combinations of letters and sounds. The word *peach* no longer sounded grating, because it didn't bring a peach to mind anymore. There was no need to think up a better name.

Sergey stretched, careful not to knock the table with his arms. "See, big enough to fit a sofa and separate from where I sleep too," Pavel had said about the kitchen in his studio. He had sublet it to Sergey, referring to it as "your room" during the transaction and "the living room" or "the kitchen" ever since.

Sergey turned onto his side so he lay facing the mangy back of the sofa, where he kept a snap-shot of his wife stuck between the pillows. He hadn't seen Lenka for almost a year, but he looked at the snapshot every day. And now, whenever

Sergey tried to call her face to mind, it was the image in the snapshot that came to him. The woman in the snapshot had the same thin nose as Lenka, the same fair brows, and the same high cheekbones, but her mouth was stretched into a tight smile, and the expression on her face was awkward and insincere. Sergey knew this wasn't Lenka's expression, but he couldn't see what her face really looked like anymore. Sometimes a fleeting memory of the pasty skin of her cheeks, or the dimple in her chin, or the beads of sweat that would speckle the tip of her nose when she moved on top of him, would appear to Sergey, but these visions were always too brief and incomplete to be satisfying. The only time he could see her whole face now was in his sleep, where she often didn't look like Lenka at all, but Sergey just knew it was her.

Other parts of her body he remembered better. Her legs were thin and pale, easily bruised, often covered in the summer with scratches and pink swellings from mosquito bites. He could see her ribs and her vertebrae when she sat smoking on the opposite side of their bed. Once he began tracing the contours of her spine with his finger, but she made him stop. She said that when she was a little girl, she had this drunk uncle who used to sit her in his lap and "count her ribs," poking his fat fingers hard between each bone. Lenka's fingers were light and cool, always light and cool. This Sergey remembered very well.

When he phoned her last night—early morning in Russia—she sighed, and yawned, and didn't say anything for a long time. He asked her if he had woken her up. "Um, no, I don't know," she mumbled. He looked at the snapshot and imagined that it was not a picture of Lenka but of some other—strange—woman, and it was this strange woman who had picked up the phone. The real Lenka, *his* Lenka, wouldn't have yawned into the phone, she would have squealed with delight at the sound of his voice, as she always did during the first couple of months after he left for America. The real Lenka would have cried, "Serionya! You!" The real Lenka would have begged him to return home sooner. "Yes, I know, I know we need the money, I know," she would say, in a light, tiny voice, quickly sounding out of breath. "But can't you do something—anything—to speed it up?"

Back in Russia, she would rush to meet him when he came home from work every night. She jumped around him like a puppy while he removed his shoes and jacket, hugging him, grabbing him by the hands, covering him with untargeted kisses. He would smile and peck her on a cheek, embarrassed to show how much her reaction stirred him, afraid to reveal his anxiety of the moments before. Every time, as he walked up the stairs leading to their apartment, he tried hard not to run, wondering if Lenka would be jumping when she saw him or if this would be the day when he came and found that something was gone, and Lenka would be clanking dishes in the kitchen or watching TV on the couch and would just nod at him when he entered the room.

The woman in the snapshot smiled at him with her mouth closed and explained in a patient schoolteacher's voice that since he had such a great job there was simply no point in his returning to Russia now. Yes, the snapshot remembered that they had decided he would go for only a year. And yes, they had saved enough money for a small apartment. But that was enough only for a very, very small one, and then they would need nice furniture and a new car, right? She told him that she missed him a lot, missed him more than he missed her, and that the separation was harder for her than for him anyway, so if she could find the strength to be patient, so could he. It was the woman in the snapshot that Sergey was angry with, in a way he had never been with the real Lenka. He shoved the snapshot farther between the cushions, sat up, and swung his legs to the floor.

There wasn't any aspirin in the bathroom medicine cabinet. None by the kitchen sink or in the clay bowl where he kept random pills found in his pockets. Sergey took a broom from the corner, shoved it under his couch, and with a generous swing produced a gray, fuzzy pile of objects. He lowered himself onto his knees, carefully, so as not to move his head too much, and examined what he had found. There—among Pavel's bottle of brandy, which Sergey had finished after last night's phone call, a months-old Russian newspaper, a telephone bill with a long string of Lenka's number broken in places by the number of Pavel's wife, three hardened socks, two emptied aspirin foils, and about a dollar fifty in change— he found a plastic snippet with two extra-strength Ibuprofens inside. He swallowed them dry, swept the rest of his finds back under the couch, and lay down.

Sergey fell asleep and dreamed of a woman's light cool fingers touching his forehead, stroking his face, dancing down his chest and stomach, getting warmer as they went.

He woke up an hour later to the sound of running water and the bang of a teakettle landing on the stove. Pavel was moving swiftly around the kitchen like a big nervous cat. "Shit, we're out of milk," Pavel said in English. Pat, Pavel's current girlfriend, slouched over a mug at the table, her bare feet hooked around the chair's legs. Pat had a ruddy complexion and wild hair dyed purplish red. *New Jersey sunset*, Sergey thought, the first time he saw her. In the mornings after she stayed overnight, Pat always wore a short white bathrobe, which made her seem even more startlingly red by contrast. Her thighs, visible to Sergey under the table, looked flushed, as if they emanated heat. Sergey turned over and closed his eyes, embarrassed by the almost painful sensation this sight produced in him.

WHEN SERGEY got up hours later to an empty apartment, he washed his face and ate a few handfuls of cornflakes right from the box. The teakettle was still warm, so Sergey poured water and instant coffee into a cup and began stirring, watching how the dark granules circled around his spoon, refusing to dissolve, and listening to the sounds of the apartment: the low buzz of the fridge, the dripping faucet, the clock ticking off each wasted second. Pavel and Pat had left a swirl of bread crumbs on the table, and Sergey could still smell the sweet scent of Pat's hand cream.

The top of the Russian newspaper Sergey had pushed back under the couch caught his eye. It was covered in sticky dust and feeble strands of brown hair, but Sergey spread it out on the table. He sipped his coffee, flipping through real estate ads with pictures of frosty, unattractive brokers, and immigrations services ads with roguish lawyers in bulky suits. He leafed through countless pictures of enormous teeth gleaming next to the names of dentists. Flipped right past the ads for oncologists, for the treatments of skin diseases and erectile dysfunction. Stopped to snort at the holistic medicine ads, which promised to cure whatever the other ads didn't. Chuckled at the ad for "an authentic witch from the woods of Western Ukraine" who claimed the ability to solve both marital and financial problems. And finally arrived at a section that dazzled him.

The naked women on the page came in various shapes and colors, yet they all had two things in common: they were visibly moaning, and stars and solid black rectangles covered their breasts and genitals. Sergey took a long swallow of coffee and tried to mentally unscrape the stars and rectangles. He imagined that he was the one who made the women moan. The words accompanying the snapshots boasted of *heavenly pleasures* and *hot, hot, hot women.* One of the ads promised time with a beautiful, blue-eyed, long-haired mermaid. Sergey imagined her cold, slimy tail, the smell of yesterday's fish at a Brighton Beach food market.

The ad he liked was small and plain, placed in the lower right corner of one of the pages: *A warm, sexy woman will tend to your needs. Affordable.* He scraped more cornflakes off the bottom of the box and read the words again, trying to hear them spoken by the woman who had placed the ad. "A warm, sexy woman will tend to your needs. Affordable." Her voice was soft but clear, and she paused slightly before *affordable*, so he knew she didn't want to humiliate him. She was expressing encouragement and understanding. This was a woman who wasn't going to torture him with longing, who wasn't trying to deceive or manipulate him, but who would tend to his needs: warmly, skillfully, quickly.

He imagined her looking like Lenka, but not the Lenka from the snapshot and not even the real Lenka—rather, a different, simpler, kinder version. Then he thought that he didn't want her to look like Lenka at all. Maybe like Pat, with her flushed thighs, or like the young cashier at the supermarket, who smiled as Sergey paid for his cereal. The trilling voice on the phone gave him a different image, however, that of a short, plump young woman with full lips and small white hands. He thought that this was exactly how he wanted her to look, not like Lenka, not like Pat. Her name was Alla. They made an appointment for six.

AT TEN OF SIX, Sergey got off the train at the Brighton Beach Avenue stop and walked down the station's metal stairs. Normally Sergey hated this street. "Stop moping and go to Brighton Beach," Pavel would tell him. "You would feel right at home." But Sergey never felt at home there. He loathed the gloomy brownstones, the loud store windows, the honking cars, the gray ocean, the cold sand the color of carpet in a New Jersey home, and the smug, well-fed people smoking by the shining doors of restaurants, picking through piles of fruit, loading heavy bags of food into the trunks of their cars. This was the fake Russia, the parody of Russia, that made the real Russia seem even farther away and hopelessly unobtainable.

But now the bustle of Brighton Beach Avenue filled Sergey with a kind of spiteful satisfaction. All those months he'd been saving every penny, thinking of every dollar as one step closer to taking him home, every thousand as one giant step. He didn't buy any clothes, he didn't accompany Pavel to bars, he stinted on everything, living on cornflakes, pasta, and an occasional chicken. And now he was about to blow so much money on this obscenely selfish thing? He felt as if he were tearing the money out of Lenka's hands and he chuckled, imagining the expression of stunned fury the snapshot-Lenka would assume if she knew. He walked onto 6th Street, turning to face the stark wind blowing in from the Atlantic.

*Borscht*

The door to Alla's four-story building was ajar, so Sergey walked up the staircase without buzzing her. The homey smells of cooking intensified and grew more complex with each flight of steep stone stairs. Sergey was able to make out onions frying in fat, boiling cabbage, garlic, a rich meat dish. By the time he reached the top floor, Alla's floor, his stomach was growling, and Sergey realized he hadn't eaten anything since this morning's dry cornflakes.

The doorbell made a short, angry buzz. Too short, or too low, because he could hear only silence behind the door. Sergey's defiant energy left him, and in its place came dread and embarrassment. He stood with his index finger suspended over the worn white buzzer, unable to press it again. He had a memory of standing just like he stood now, useless and ridiculous, in front of a woman's door back in Russia, his hands busy with a dripping bouquet and a carton with cake as he pressed the doorbell with his shoulder. He felt naked without the cake and the bouquet and wished he had something to offer other than the four twenty-dollar bills in his pocket. He was about to turn and leave when he heard approaching steps and the door opened.

The hall was dim, and it took Sergey's eyes a moment to adjust, before he was able to make out the form and face of the woman. She was stocky, with a red, wrinkled neck, blotchy face, and smudges of mascara in deep creases around her eyes. Her short hair, dyed black and highlighted with dandelion yellow, was gathered into a bristly ponytail. "Hello, I'm Alla," she said, extending her hand for a shake.

As he stepped toward her, Sergey felt woozy, almost panicky, with disappointment. It was hot in the apartment, with a thick smell of cooking, and his head started to ache again. "Nice to meet you," he mumbled, taking her damp, puffy hand in his.

"I'm not dressed yet," Alla said, and began untying the flowery apron she wore over a purple T-shirt and blue track-suit pants. "I just need to turn the stove off. You, Sergey, go into the bedroom, relax, take your jacket off." When Sergey was already heading down the hallway, she asked him to take off his shoes. "This is Masha's apartment, not mine. She has carpet everywhere."

Sergey made a stop in the bathroom, where he combed his hair and tried to pee. His head was starting to pound. Maybe he could tell Alla that he had a headache and leave, but then he thought how ridiculous this excuse would sound. He opened the medicine cabinet and found a container of Tylenol behind a disarray of near-empty nail polish bottles. He swallowed two pills, washed them down with water from the faucet, wiped his chin with his hands, wiped his hands against his pants, and trudged to the bedroom.

Alla was already there, crouched in front of the closet, looking for something on the bottom shelf. "Sit down, make yourself at home," she said to Sergey. He took his jacket off, wondering if his armpits stank, and sat on the edge of the bed. The carpet in the room was unusually dark, a color called, as Sergey knew, *Smashed blueberry.* He tried to cheer himself up by thinking of a better name but couldn't come up with anything other than *Blood turning blue.* The room was cluttered with dark polished chests, some adorned with crystal vases, others with large framed photographs of a bosomy blonde without a neck. Masha, Sergey guessed. Masha liked to be photographed in restaurants, hugging a sickly-looking bald man and raising a champagne glass in her hand.

"We can take care of the money now," Alla said, having emerged from the closet with some bright, crumpled clothes spilling over her arms. Sergey saw a red bra, a pink tag still attached to it on a thread.

"That'd be seventy-five dollars. I always say, Money first."

Sergey felt a fleeting relief. This was the part of the procedure that he didn't doubt he could perform. He reached into a pocket of his jeans and took out his four slightly crumpled twenties.

Alla put the clothes onto the bed, took the money, and counted it. Then she sighed and looked at Sergey. "I don't think I have any small bills to give you your five bucks back."

"That's all right," Sergey said.

She nodded and put the money into a drawer.

"Do you like rock music?" Alla asked next. He said that he didn't mind it.

"I'll put something on for you while I'm changing." She pressed buttons on a battered stereo system, picked up her clothes, and disappeared into the bathroom.

Sergey was prepared to be hit with heavy metal or hard rock, but he heard instead, after a scratchy silence, the intro to "Heartbreak Hotel." His feet were tapping against the carpet when he heard the toilet flush, and suddenly he became aware that Alla was just a few steps away from him, changing. He imagined her fastening her brand-new bra and then bending over the sink to apply fresh mascara. Lenka put her mascara on while bending over the sink in only panties and a bra. But he didn't want to think about Lenka now. Lenka was far away, and getting farther every day. Alla was right here. Sergey shifted on the bed, stirred by the certainty of what was about to happen.

But when Alla finally emerged from the bathroom, wearing silver sandals, a black miniskirt, and a dark-red shimmering blouse, it seemed too soon to Sergey. Her lips were thickly smeared with plum lipstick and contoured with a darker shade of plum. She looked heavy, uncomfortable, and aggressive. Sergey's head began to throb harder, as if it were gathering the strength to fight off two Tylenols.

Alla asked him something, but he couldn't hear her over the music.

"What do you want?" she repeated, trying to outshout Elvis.

Sergey didn't know what to say. The truth was that he wanted it any possible way, but not now and not with Alla.

"I personally prefer blow jobs," Alla said. "Quick, easy, and no mess afterward. Do you want a blow job?" Sergey nodded, thinking that the blow job had two obvious advantages: he wouldn't have to do anything, and he wouldn't have to see a lot of Alla while she was at it.

But instead of approaching him, Alla stepped back into the narrow space between the bed and the chest of drawers and snapped her fingers to the intro to "One Night with You." When Elvis began singing, she started dancing. Her thin, short legs looked wobbly as her high heels sank into the carpet. Her hips swayed back and forth and her head bobbed. She occasionally would turn away from Sergey, doing something to her blouse.

He noticed that each time she turned back to him she had undone one more button. Her breasts weren't large, not even filling the cups of her new red bra, but the straps were fastened too tight, so that the material cut deep into the flabby yellow flesh of her stomach and shoulders. The color of dead chicken, Sergey thought, as Alla stepped closer and closer to him. He wondered if it would be rude to shut his eyes, then shut them anyway, just as Alla knelt before him on the carpet.

Sergey wasn't sure how much time—filled with rough sensations, waves of Alla's sharply sour smell, images of huge human teeth closing around him, and the pounding music—passed before Alla finally let him go and moved her head away. Could have been five minutes or fifty. "What's wrong?" she asked Sergey, out of breath. "Are you feeling okay?" Her face was sweaty and red, with lipstick smudges on her chin. She massaged her jaw and moved her stiffened neck left and right.

Sergey's whole body felt long and empty, drained of energy, incapable of anything except producing a headache, which was now throbbing even harder.

"I better go," Sergey said, zipping up his pants.

"Maybe you need to rest a little?"

Sergey shook his head.

"Are you feeling sick or something? Because I did everything well, right? It's not my fault?"

"No, it's not your fault; I have a headache," he said, avoiding her stare.

"Headache? Do you want some Tylenol? I've got some in the bathroom."

"No, I'm okay. I just took some." He needed to leave, but Alla had scrambled to her feet and was blocking his way.

"I don't have to give you your money back, right? Since it's not my fault."

"No. No, you don't."

She let Sergey pass but followed him into the hallway, buttoning her blouse as they went and wiping her chin with the back of her hand.

"You know what? I'll give you your five bucks back, then. I might have change in my purse after all."

"No, that's okay."

Sergey reached for his shoes. He felt a momentary sting about the money, muffled by the desire to leave this place. Right away. Run down the stairs, push open the exit door, and take gulps of cold ocean air.

"Maybe you want a glass of water or something? Some juice? I've got some currant juice."

Sergey shook his head, quickly lacing his shoes.

And then as he stood to leave, Alla caught him by a sleeve.

"I know what I'll give you. Some borscht! You can't say no to a bowl of borscht, right?"

In the bedroom, Elvis drew out the last stammering note and the cassette ended with a snap.

ALLA SEATED Sergey at the kitchen table and went to turn on the gas under a large enamel pot.

"Won't take long, don't worry. We have to let it simmer for five minutes or so," she told Sergey.

Alla moved the lid a little bit so that only the slightest puffs of steam could escape, then broke a clove off a head of garlic sitting on the windowsill and grabbed a bunch of parsley that was hanging upside down from a cabinet handle.

Alla peeled the garlic clove, cut it in half, and chopped it up. She had changed and was now wearing a fresh white T-shirt over the same track-suit pants he saw before. Most of the makeup had been washed off her face, which made her look both rougher and younger. Sergey marveled at how light and fast her fingers were.

"Do you want a shot of something, Sergey? Masha's husband has a whole collection of infused vodkas."

"Thank you," Sergey said, "but I don't drink."

"At all?"

"It gives me headaches."

"Well, I can't drink either. I have to go to work in a couple of hours."

"I thought you worked here."

Alla froze, the knife suspended in midair.

"Here? What do you mean *here*? What do you think I am, some kind of a prostitute? I work as a nanny in Manhattan!"

Sergey mumbled an apology, and Alla calmed down enough to resume chopping.

"They are a very good family. Americans. He's a lawyer, and she used to be something too. But now she does her projects, that's her word—'Alla, I have a lot of projects today'—and I watch the kids. She loves me, because I speak a little English and don't mind doing the cleaning and the laundry. She says their previous nanny didn't speak any English at all, and the one before her knew only two words: *No laundry*."

She mixed the garlic and parsley together on the cutting board, sprinkled them with salt, and chopped them up.

"I live with them too. But Masha—she's a really good friend; we go way back—said I could stay with her on my days off so I could take a break from them, you know. To rest, to sleep, to cook some real food. There used to be this other woman, Lubka; she rented a room from Masha, and it was her business. Then she found another job and moved out, and Masha offered me the room to take over. 'God sees,' she said. 'You're better looking than Lubka.'"

Alla paused, probably expecting a confirmation of her better looks, but since Sergey had never seen Lubka, he didn't know what to say.

"What do you do, Sergey?"

"I install carpets."

"Oh, that's a nice job too. I hear they pay well."

Alla opened the lid on the pot with the borscht and fished out four large pink potatoes. "I cook them whole in my borscht, then take them out and crush them. My mother and my aunts all used to do it like that."

She carried the steaming bowl to the table and prodded the potatoes with a large fork. "Well, not as fluffy as in Russia, but still nice and soft. You have to crush them, not mash them. I don't know why, but they say it's important." She stuck her fork in and broke the soft yellow flesh of the potato, leaving four furrows in its surface.

"You know what, Sergey? Why don't you slice the bread while I'm doing this?"

She took a dark brick of rye bread out of a bread box and handed it to Sergey along with a cutting board and a long steel knife. The bread had such a fresh, heady smell that Sergey couldn't resist breaking the crust of the first slice and stuffing it into his mouth.

"It's a nice knife, isn't it?" Alla asked.

Sergey nodded. "Did you bring it from Russia?"

"Masha. Masha did. She came to stay, so she shipped a whole bunch of stuff here: plates, knives, cutting boards, bowls. Even—listen to this—even a basin for washing clothes! Can you believe this? A basin for washing clothes!" She laughed, and so did Sergey.

"What about you, Alla? Are you here to stay?"

"Me? No way! My family's there. My husband, my girls."

Sergey stared at her. "You're married?"

"Why wouldn't I be? I've been married for eighteen years, not counting another two when I was married to my first husband."

She turned to point to the cluster of snapshots clipped to the refrigerator with banana magnets. Most of them pictured two young women and a stocky mustached man.

"What about you, Sergey? Are you staying?"

"No. I came only for a year. To work."

"And how much of the year is left?"

"Actually, I was supposed to be heading back by now, but then we decided, my wife and I, that I might stay a little longer. You know, since I'm making good money here."

"Oh, I know, I know. I know this song by heart. 'Don't worry, Mom, we manage fine here.' And they do, they do manage fine without me, as long as the money's coming. 'Of course I miss you, Alla, but you better stay as long as your visa is good.'"

She took the bowl with crushed potatoes and carefully slipped them into the pot.

"Think about it, Serezha. He used to bring me coffee in bed when we first got married. Coffee in bed! That's how crazy he was about me. And then suddenly it was all gone. How, when? Once, a few years ago, I was readying myself for a party— dressing up: earrings, perfume, mascara—and my husband walked into the room and squinted at me from the corner. 'Remember, Alla,' he said, 'what a heavenly beauty you used to be?'"

She paused and looked at Sergey. He felt he should say something to her but didn't know what.

"Yeah, just like that. But what can I say? Life is life, and the only way to live it is to take all the shit that comes with it."

She stirred the borscht and put the lid back on.

"How long have you been married, may I ask?"

"Eighteen months."

"Eighteen months! And you spent twelve of them living apart! Saving for an apartment?"

"Yes."

"Me too. For two apartments. One so my oldest daughter could divorce her husband, and another so the youngest could get married."

Alla went to the refrigerator and pulled the snapshots of her daughters from their banana clips.

"See here, Serezha," she said, carefully placing the pictures in front of him. "This is Natasha, my oldest, very nice girl, quiet, serious, smart, not at all like her *papik*—alcoholic. She is my daughter from my first marriage, and my current husband never really warmed up to her—which could be a good thing, some people say to me. But that's why Natashka married that jerk at eighteen. Didn't want to live with us. He drinks, he cheats, and he doesn't work—exactly the three worst things about a husband—and poor Natashka got all three. My husband at least has a job. She would've gotten a divorce, but there is no place to live."

Alla sighed and picked up another snapshot.

"And here is Marinka, the young one. Pretty, right? Too pretty, if you ask me. She's been hanging out with boys ever since she turned fifteen. All I want is for her to marry and settle down. But again, she would need a place to live."

Alla put the snapshots down on the table and went to take a plastic container with sour cream out of the refrigerator. She then put two deep plates and two silver spoons on the two ends of the table and placed a wooden trivet in the middle.

Sergey brought the pictures closer to his eyes. Alla was right—Marinka was very pretty. Pert, muscular, with dark eyes and dark hair, her laughing face glowing with wild energy. She was the kind of girl with whom you'd want to wrestle in bed. Sergey had a quick image of himself grabbing her wrists, pinning her down, and her kicking and laughing. But Natasha was very pretty too, although her beauty seemed to be softer, less aggressive, less obvious from the first glance. She was the kind of girl you'd want to kiss while walking with her in a park. She didn't resemble her sister at all, except for her long dark eyes, which looked exactly like Marinka's and, Sergey noticed with surprise, like Alla's.

"Your daughters are beautiful, and they both look like you," Sergey said.

Alla looked at him from the stove and smiled, "Thank you, Serezha."

And then the hot borscht was in their plates. Steaming, bursting with colors. All shades of red in perfect harmony with the faded purple of beets, the deep orange of fat rings, the white of sour cream in the middle, and the dark green of parsley bits.

"You know what?" Alla said, as they were

about to plunge their spoons in. "We simply have to have some of Masha's vodka now."

She opened the freezer, and Sergey smiled at the bright collection of colorful, translucent liquids in half-liter bottles on the three upper shelves.

"Ash berry is the best one. Masha's husband drove upstate specially to gather the berries."

Sergey poured about a finger of faint amber liquid into each of two shot glasses.

"We have to make a toast," Alla said, and looked into her glass. "For going home? No matter if they're waiting for us or not?"

"For going home," Sergey said, and they clinked their glasses.

He felt a chill on his tongue followed by a great immediate warmth spreading down his throat and chest. He took a big heavy spoonful of borscht and brought it to his mouth, holding a piece of bread under the spoon.

# Puffed Rice and Meatballs

$O$NCE, in a hazy postcoital silence, Katya's lover came back from a shower, dropped the towel to the floor, climbed into bed, and said, "Tell me about your childhood. Tell me about the horrors of communism."

Katya sat hugging her knees so that her body resembled a triangle with her head as an apex. She had put on her bra and panties—she hated nakedness, how it turned into something sadly irrelevant after sex.

The request startled her. What exactly were the horrors of communism? Katya's childhood coincided with the Stagnation Period. People weren't killed or put in prisons as easily as before, there was plenty of space in mental hospitals, and—as for the freedoms of speech, residence, and such—what did little Katya need them for? Was having to wear a red tie horrible, or standing in a two-hour line to see Lenin's body in his tomb, or standing in an even longer line to buy toilet paper? Katya didn't think so. It was rather funny. Even nostalgic now. And why would a man with whom she'd gone on only a few dates and exchanged a few embraces be interested in something as intimate as her childhood?

She stared at her lover suspiciously.

He had propped up his head with his elbow. His expression was of calm anticipation. This man didn't want to know her better. He was simply asking for entertainment—for an easy, amusing, and preferably sexy story about the exotic world to which his lover had once belonged. Katya's shoulders relaxed.

After some mental probing she picked a story. She wasn't sure if it had anything to do with communism, but she thought that with a few effective details she would be able to make the narrative exotic enough. She put her right cheek on her knee and turned to her lover.

"Do you want to hear about my first sexual encounter?"

"Gladly!"

"When I was little, I attended a day-long preschool, like most city kids. We were on a very strict schedule, similar to a prison or a labor camp. Every day, at one P.M., we had a nap. Our teacher—I remember only that she had red ears and a long lumpy nose—put us in two lines and led us to the bedroom, a gloomy room where the blinds were drawn at all times and the beds stood in tight rows, a girl's bed alternating with a boy's."

"I see," Katya's lover noted with enthusiasm. "So you were sandwiched between two boys."

"Not exactly. Between a boy and a wall, because my bed was the last in a row.

"We stripped to our underwear—boys and girls had identical white underpants and undershirts—climbed into the beds, pulled the blankets to our chins, and turned to the right side. We weren't allowed to sleep on our backs or our left sides. As soon as we all were in bed, the teacher said, 'I'm going now, but if I hear even a squeak from you, I'm coming back, and I'm coming back with *the thing*!' Nobody knew what *the thing* was, and nobody wanted to find out.

"'And if you go to the bathroom, it better be an emergency!' she added before leaving for the dining room.

"I couldn't sleep on my right side. I just lay there scared and bored, facing the back of the boy next to me, staring at his blanket's ornament through the rectangular slit in the blanket cover.

"Delicious sounds coming from the dining room distracted me even more. I listened to the plates clatter and the persistent scraping of a serving spoon against a pot's bottom. I knew that in a few minutes the teacher would open the entrance door and let in her sons, twin boys of about nine. She would seat them at our tables and feed them the food left over from our lunch. I saw them once, when I pleaded an emergency and ran through the dining room to the bathroom. Their plates were piled up with shrunken meat-balls and pale mounds of mashed potatoes. Their knees were bent awkwardly under one of our little-kids' tables. Their ears moved along with their jaws.

"I tossed in bed and thought about meatballs, which during naptime always seemed awfully tempting, even though I'd repeatedly refused them during lunch. 'Want to be hungry? Fine,' the teacher had said, hastily taking away my plate. 'This school is no place for picky eaters.'"

Katya's lover listened with a warm and amused expression, tinted with slight shadows of impatience. She didn't know why she'd mentioned the teacher's boys at all. She'd better hurry up and get to the sex part.

She continued her story. "A thin voice from the next bed interrupted my meatball fantasies. 'Hey, are you asleep?' The voice belonged to a chunky blue-eyed boy named Vova. He had turned toward me and lay blinking with his white eyelashes.

"'Can't you see that my eyes are open?' I asked.

"'Shh.' He pointed in the dining room's direction. The white eyelashes blinked some more. 'I'll show you my *peesya* if you show me yours.'

"I didn't have any problems with that. We moved our blankets aside and pulled down our underpants. We craned our necks. We stared.

"'Mine's better,' Vova said at last.

"I agreed. His was better. His looked like something you could play with.

"'It's so pretty and small,' I said.

That was the only time I didn't lie about a man's size, Katya wanted to add, but then changed her mind.

"'What do you do with it?'

"'Not much, really.' He shrugged, tucking his *peesya* into his underpants. 'I pee with it; I pull on it sometimes. Not much.'

"'Not much?' I frowned. Such a pretty, fun toy. I would have known what to do with it! For one thing I would've dressed it in all the clothes from my tiny-dolls collection. I would've tried little hats, socks, and dresses on it. Then I would've tried to feed it and put it into bed."

"Classic case of penis envy," Katya's lover said, laughing. He was playing with her bra straps.

"Oh, no, not at all. I didn't feel envy. It was rather a feeling of waste that such a promising thing wasn't properly used.

"Anyway, I was excited, and I couldn't wait to go home and tell my mother. In fact, I didn't wait to go home. I told her on the way from school. I stopped in the middle of a dry summer sidewalk, let go of my mother's hand, and said, 'Mom, you won't believe what I saw today!'

"Several hours of yelling, sobbing, and hysterical phone confessions to her friends followed. Then there was a lecture. My mother led me into a room that we shared—my little bed stood perpendicularly to her big one—sat me on a little chair in the corner, and walked to the middle of the room, her arms folded on her chest and her brows furrowed. I think I might have giggled, because I remember my mother suddenly yelling, 'It's not funny! It's a very serious matter!'

"The lecture wasn't long. I remember sitting patiently through the whole of it, and I couldn't have possibly done that if the lecture lasted more than twenty minutes. At one point my mother began to sob in mid-sentence and ran to lock herself in the bathroom."

"Oh, my God. It could've left you scarred for life."

Katya stopped. Her lover looked mildly horrified. He'd even freed his fingers from under the straps of her bra.

It would be a bad idea to mention that she then had banged on the bathroom door, yelling, "Mommy, please, please forgive me!" It would be an even worse idea to add that she had dropped to her knees and tried to calm her mother by whispering through the slit under the door. The last thing Katya needed was to show her scars.

She continued in a lighter tone.

"After my mother had gone, I decided to go on with the lecture. Probably wanted to try on the role of an authority figure. I gathered all my dolls—some I had to pull from under the beds and bookcases—and sat them on little chairs from my toy furniture set. It was a peculiar group, with the dolls ranging from one inch to three feet high, a few with missing body parts. 'Listen to me,' I said, looming above them with my arms folded on my chest. 'Listen hard, you bunch of stupid, irresponsible dolls. And don't you giggle! Never ever show your little *peesya* to anyone. First of all, good dolls don't do that. Second of all, you can go to prison for it.'"

Katya paused before the punch line.

"And guess what? They never did."

The punch line worked, lifting Katya's lover's hands back to her bra straps and making him laugh.

"But you did. You did! You weren't as obedient as your dolls."

"No, I wasn't," Katya agreed, and helped to unhook her bra.

The story was a success. It was certainly better than watching the news broadcast, as they did the last time. "You were great," he had said, pulling on his socks afterward, but she wasn't sure whether he referred to their lovemaking or her patience in watching the news.

IT WASN'T until much later, when Katya returned to her Brooklyn apartment, that the story started to bother her. It felt like the onset of a toothache, a vague gnawing sensation that would grow into real pain at any moment. Katya brewed some bitter dark tea right in the mug and opened a jar of walnut jam, which, having cost her a ridiculous $5.99, still didn't taste like home. It was too sugary—wrong—just like her story. The very lightness of her carefully dispensed jokes made her shiver with disgust now. It's not funny! she wanted to scream, like her mother had. Her mother, whom she'd just betrayed for a strange man's entertainment.

Soon Katya was awash with shame: for herself, for her mother, but most of all for the hungry teacher's boys who had to eat leftovers at the little kids' tables.

At the bottom of her mug sat a small pile of tea leaves, the very stuff people used to read to tell fortunes. Years ago Katya did that with her best friend, Vera. They sat leaning over their mugs, the tip of Katya's yellow braid touching the table.

"I don't see anything," Vera complained. "I see a shape," Katya said. "A shape of what? A man?" Katya shrugged. "A shape of something."

She peered into the pile now and tried to read if she would ever meet a man who would understand her pity and her shame, to whom she'd tell her real stories, the ones that mattered, the ones that haunted her, without dressing them up with descriptions of labor-camp preschool, her red tie, or her family's lack of bread and toilet paper.

"There were two things I craved as a child: imported clothes and imported junk food in crunchy bags." That was how she would start her real story.

One day I came close to having them both.

It happened soon after I turned thirteen. I remember the year exactly, because it was the year when I developed breasts, and it was also the year when my aunt Marusya returned from West Germany and brought me a bunch of hip German clothes. "Here, dig in!" she said, handing me a tightly packed plastic bag.

I ran to my room and shook the bag's contents right onto the floor. They made an impressive pile. I wanted to dive in and swim in that colorful sea of fabric. Instead, I sat in the middle of the pile and ran the clothes through my fingers, like somebody who'd opened a treasure box. I stretched stockings, I stroked fuzzy sweaters, I played with shiny metallic belts. I even kissed one nylon blouse that I particularly liked. Then I hurried to try everything on, afraid that if I waited, they might disappear. I pulled them on, one by one, admiring my reflection in the shiny glass shelves of the bookcase. The clothes, though obscured by book covers, looked divine, even more than divine—they looked just like the ones in the dog-eared J.C. Penney catalog I'd once seen at my best friend Vera's place.

The last piece in the pile was a modest beige sweater with funny shoulder straps. Why would somebody sew shoulder straps to a sweater? I'd thought, when I first saw it. And why bother spending precious currency, when you could buy a simple thing like that here? But I was wrong, I was very wrong, and I saw it as soon as I tried the sweater on. That pale unimpressive piece of cloth could perform miracles. I didn't know whether it was because of the shoulder straps or some other tailoring trick, but it made me appear as if I had breasts! I couldn't believe my eyes. For several months I'd been staring into the bathroom mirror hoping to discover the much-desired swellings on my chest. I kneaded and pinched myself, but no matter how hard I tried, it didn't work. My chest was as flat and as hard as my grandmother's washboard. Drink more milk, my happier, breast-equipped girlfriends advised. I did. I drank six to eight glasses a day, fighting the spasms of nausea. It didn't work.

And now here they were: two soft little knobs pushing against the beige fabric. They were my very real breasts. They were beautiful. The girl who blinked at me from the bookcase's surface was beautiful. She was not just pretty or cute, as people mistakenly called her. She was strikingly, undeniably beautiful. Apparently, the beauty had always been there, but buried under the wrong clothes.

I had to show the world.

I dialed Vera's number and asked her to meet me by the playground.

I threw on a new miniskirt and new tights and ran to the door, past my parents, who were getting drunk on foreign liquor and Aunt Marusya's stories of foreign life.

Clomping down the steps of the littered staircase, I suddenly thought of my newfound beauty as a burden. Being beautiful couldn't be easy. It could be troublesome and even embarrassing. People would stare at me now; I would produce some reaction in the outside world, make some change. And I would have to react. But how? How exactly did a beautiful person behave? What was I supposed to do when boys stared at me and at my breasts, which I was certain they would? I had a surge of titillating panic as I opened the entrance door and stopped, blinded by the orange rays of the setting sun.

I'd just keep my eyes down, I decided. I'd let them stare, but I'd keep my eyes down.

Vera presented a bigger problem. Would it be possible to stay friends? Vera, with her flat square face and thick waist, wasn't even pretty, let alone beautiful, and about eighty percent of our conversations had consisted of berating the stupid and boy-crazy pretty girls. Yet she'd been my best friend for years, and I didn't want to lose her.

She loped toward me now, swinging a canvas bag in one hand and waving a wad of money with the other. Was she ungraceful! I slouched and messed up my hair, trying to make my beauty a little less obvious.

But when Vera drew near, I saw that my worries were in vain. Her forehead was covered with sweat and her eyes bulged with excitement; she clearly was oblivious to everything in the world, including the sudden beauty of her friend.

"Puffed . . . puffed . . . puffed rice," she panted. "They are selling puffed rice in the Littlestore." She clutched my sleeve and tried to catch a breath. "American puffed rice in crunchy bags! A friend of my mother's hairdresser told us. We have to run because the line is getting bigger every second."

"But I don't have any money!"

"I'll lend you some."

And we loped in the store's direction together.

We were two hundred fifty-sixth and two hundred fifty-seventh in the line. The reason we knew was that they scribbled the numbers in blue ink right on our palms. I had to keep my marked hand apart, so the number wouldn't rub off accidentally, as happened to a woman who stood ahead of us. She kept showing her sweaty palm to everybody and asking if they could still read her number, when there wasn't anything but a faded blue stain. I was sure they would turn her away from the counter. The subjects of clothes, boys, and beauty lost their importance somehow, or maybe it was just hard to think of such nonsense while guarding your marked hand.

The line moved slowly. Everybody shifted from one foot to the other, waiting to take a step forward. They were admitting people in batches of ten or twelve—as many as could fit into the narrow aisle of the store.

I chewed on my ponytail. Vera rolled and unrolled the ruble bills in her hand. We were too tired to talk, as were other people. All eyes focused on the exit door, where the happy ones squeezed by with armfuls of crunchy silver-and-yellow bags. The people looked shabby and crumpled, but the bags shone winningly in the orange rays of the sun.

"Let's buy two each," Vera suggested, when the line advanced to the one hundreds. I nodded. She smoothed the crumpled ruble bills in her hand. There were five of them: enough to buy ten bags of puffed rice or two bags and a round can of instant coffee in the Bigstore next door, as Vera's mother had suggested. I thought what a good friend Vera was. Another person would've just spent all the money, without sharing it with me. I asked myself if I would've done the same thing for Vera. I wasn't sure.

"Let's buy six," Vera said, when we advanced to the store doors. I nodded.

She reached with her hand and touched a bag of puffed rice in somebody's arms. It crunched just as I'd expected.

"You know what? Let's buy ten," Vera decided. I nodded.

My feet hurt and my lips were parched. But instead of craving a drink, I craved dry and salty puffed rice.

We stood just a few people away from the doors now. They'd let us in with the next batch! Only a little while longer before I could feel the crunchy surface of a bag in my hands, before I could rip it open, before I could let the golden avalanche pour into my hand. I licked a trickle of saliva off the corner of my mouth.

Then a saleswoman appeared in the doorway.

"Seven o'clock. The store is closed," she said.

For a few moments, nobody moved. Nobody made a sound. People just stood gazing at the woman intently, as if she spoke a foreign language and they were struggling to interpret her words. Then the crowd erupted. The feeble, polite pleas grew into demands, then into curses, then into an angry, unintelligible murmur.

The woman listened with a tired and annoyed expression. She shook her head and pulled on the door. She wore a white apron and a white hat above thin dark hair gathered in a loose bun. She had a smooth, round birthmark on the right side of her chin. I'd never hated anybody as much as I hated her. My hands clenched into fists. I prepared to punch her in the face. Even though I had never done it before, I knew exactly what it would be like. I heard the swishing sound of my striking arm and her scream. I saw the thin skin of her cheeks breaking under my knuckles. I saw her blood. I saw her sink to the floor. Then I realized it was somebody else who had punched her.

Almost immediately I felt a strong shove in the back and found myself swimming inside the store. I was squeezed between other bodies and I was going in. I was going in! In! We were storming the store. Just like the crowd that was storming the Czar's Palace in all of the revolution movies. Only now I was more than the audience. I was a part of the crowd.

There was a drunken determination on people's faces. We crashed through the entrance and the last thing I saw on the outside was Vera, who had been pushed away.

"Vera!" I yelled halfheartedly, because in my toxic excitement I didn't really care whether she'd make it or not.

Soon I found myself pushed to the very back of the store, next to the cracked plywood door that led to the storage area. I was squeezed in among twenty or thirty people filling the tiny space between the entrance and the back door. There wasn't any puffed rice around, but I was sure they had more in storage.

"Bring it out, you bitch! We won't leave," piercing voices screamed behind me. I wiggled to turn away from the door and see what was happening.

The saleswoman had scrambled onto her knees and stood by the entrance holding her cheek. Her face flinched with a cold hatred.

"Ivan, Vasyok!" she called in a tired voice. "Where the hell are you? Call the police!"

People kept pushing. An old man to my left

shoved me between my ribs with his elbow, somebody hit me in the stomach, somebody stepped on
my foot, the light hair of a woman in front of me
stuck to my sweaty forehead.

The excitement had faded. All I wanted was
to get out. I looked for the slightest opening
between people's bodies, where I could sneak
through. There wasn't any.

Then a man appeared, either Vasyok or Ivan.
He pushed through the plywood door and
stopped right behind me. I managed to turn my
head sideways to look at him. He wasn't tall,
rather broad and heavy like my grandmother's
commode. He smiled.

"Why are you standing there like an idiot?"
the saleswoman screamed. "Do something! Call
the police!"

Vasyok or Ivan snorted.

"Why police? No need for police." He rolled up
his sleeves and smiled again. His arms were red
and perfectly round, with pale hairs scattered
between scars and tattoos.

He drew some air in and huffed into my neck.
His breath was hot and garlicky wet.

I screamed.

"No need for police," Vasyok repeated, in the
same calm and cheerful tone.

And then he lifted me off the ground. It was
the first thing that I noticed—the sensation of

being in the air, of losing control. His hands were on my chest, right there where I'd felt the precious little knobs just a couple of hours earlier. His index fingers crushed my nipples flat, while his thumbs pressed into my back, an inch away from my shoulder blades. Half crazy with fear and pain, I kicked with my knees, which was exactly what he needed. He used me as a battering ram, crashing me into the crowd to push people out of the store.

I don't remember how long it took him to clear the room. I don't remember at which point my feet met the ground, and whether I fell or not. It is strange, but I don't even remember if Vera was waiting for me at the store doors or if I had to walk home alone. I don't remember if I walked or ran.

I do remember that after changing into my pajamas that night, I took the new sweater, folded it several times, and shoved it into the garbage pail between an empty sour cream container and a long string of potato peel. And I remember thinking that I wasn't beautiful and never would be.

Later, when I lay in bed trying to fall asleep, I heard the rumble of a refuse chute—my mother was sending the garbage down. I pressed my face into the pillow and sobbed, suddenly regretting that I'd thrown the sweater away.

# Puffed Rice and Meatballs

.   .   .

KATYA PEERED into her mug again. The tea leaves looked like a bunch of dead flies. They didn't show the face of a man, nor did they give any hint of his name. If they knew something, they certainly kept it secret. Katya put the mug away and went to brush her teeth.

# Salad Olivier

MY MOTHER has always removed her shoes under the table, placed her feet on top of them, and entertained herself by curling and uncurling her toes. Aunt Masha liked to scratch her ankles with her stiletto heels. Uncle Boris stomped his right foot when he argued. "I insist!" he would say, and his hard leather heel went *boom!* against the linoleum floor. My father's feet weren't particularly funny, except when he wore mismatched socks, as he often did.

We, my cousin Violetta and I, liked to spend holiday meals under the table. From there, hidden behind three layers of tablecloth, we watched the secret life of the adult feet and listened to adult conversations.

"Mm, mm," they said, above our heads. "The salad is good today! Not bad, is it? Not bad at all!"

They champed, they crunched, they jingled their forks, they clinked glasses.

"In Paris they serve Olivier without meat," Uncle Boris said.

"Come on!"

"They do!"—angry *boom* of Uncle Boris's right shoe—"I read it in *A Moveable Feast.*"

"Olivier can't possibly be made without meat!" My mother's toes curled. "It's even worse than Olivier with bologna."

"Olivier with bologna is plebeian." Aunt Masha's stiletto heels agreed.


IF I GIGGLED, Cousin Violetta covered my mouth with her cupped hand. She had rough fingers, hardened by piano lessons. Her mother also took her to drawing and figure-skating lessons. She said that her figure-skating teacher liked to bend the kids' backs to the point where their vertebrae were about to break loose and scatter onto the rink. Poor Cousin Violetta. I didn't have to take any lessons because my father was the genius of the family. "The Mikhail Lanzman," people said about him. He used up piles of paper, covering it with formulas; he often froze with a perplexed expression during meals and conversations, and he did every simple chore slowly and zealously. When we all prepared Salad Olivier and my father sliced potatoes, he did exactly four cuts across and six lengthwise.

At that time I tried to copy him. My mother put a sofa cushion on my chair, so I could reach the table, and gave me a bowl of peeled eggs— a safer ingredient that wouldn't soil my holiday clothes. I didn't mind, even though Cousin Violetta had been trusted with sour pickles. I liked eggs. They were soft, smooth, and easy to slice.

I held an egg between my thumb and index finger, carefully counted the cuts. My father, who sat across from me, nodded approvingly. From time to time his reading glasses would slide to the tip of his nose, and it was my job to push them up because I had the cleanest hands. "Puppy Tail!" he would call, and I would slip off my pillow and rush to his end of the table, push the glasses to the bridge of his nose, and command, "Stay there!" But invariably the glasses slid down again, often as soon as I made it back to my place and resumed counting.

By the time I could reach the table without the pillow, my slicing zeal had cooled off. Strangely enough, it coincided with a vague suspicion that my father was an ordinary man after all. Ordinary, and maybe even boring. The puppy tail stopped wagging.

By the time we moved to America my cutting zeal had perished altogether.

.  .  .

"SLICE, DON'T CHOP!" my mother says in our Brooklyn kitchen. I remove the large potato chunks that I'd just put into the crystal bowl and slice them some more.

It's June 14, our first American anniversary. We'll celebrate it alone, the three of us, consuming a bowl of Olivier and a bottle of sickly sweet wine that rests on top of the refrigerator. We are not happy. In my mother's opinion, it's my fault.

"You can't say that you don't meet men. You work with men, don't you?" My mother rips sinew out of the chunks of boiled pork.

I raise my eyes. I work in a urologist's office and my mother knows it.

"Mother, the men I meet are either impotent or carry sexually transmitted diseases." This isn't completely true. The urologist also has two or three incontinence cases and a few prostate cancers, which I neglect to mention.

She purses her lips and starts knocking with her knife against the cutting board. She works fast when she is angry. The bits of meat fly from under her knife all over the table. I pick the bits up and throw them into the garbage, seeing a corner of the living room with my father's small figure sprawled on the couch. His feet, clad in perfectly matched gray socks, are placed on top of the arm-rest. His feet are the first thing I see on entering the apartment. Sometimes he taps with them rhythmically as if listening to a sad, slow tune; at other times they just stay perched there like two lost birds.

His feet were the first thing I saw yesterday, having returned from a date that had started with my mother's phone hunt for a "suitable boy" and ended with the "suitable boy" telling me I could be certain that he would never ever ask me out again.

"He's not our kind, Ma. I'm sure that in his family they put bologna in the salad," I said, try-ing to console her. She didn't buy it.

THE FACT IS, Marochka, that Tanya does have suitors," she says on the phone. "Wonderful men. But *Americans*! You understand me, don't you? There are differences that can't be resolved, dif-ferent cultures and such. We want a Russian boy for her."

I listen from the kitchen, while scraping the salad remains off the sides of the bowl.

As the call progresses, CUNY becomes NYU, the linguistic department becomes medical school, and my receptionist service at the urolo-gist's becomes my medical work. When she sees

me look over at her, my mother throws me a defiant look.

I know, I agree. If I were worthier, she
wouldn't have had to lie.

She ends the call, with "I see," followed by
"Yes, please, if you hear anything." The receiver
falls onto the base with a helpless clunk.

Then she walks into the kitchen and pours
herself a glass of currant juice. Don't pity me, she
seems to be saying, while slurping the red liquid.
It's not me who has just been rejected, it's you. I
dated enough in my time. I found a man to marry.
Her black mascara melts together with tears and
runs in tiny twisted streams down her cheeks.

At times I want to shrink so I can hug my
mother's knees, press my face against her warm
thighs, and cry with her, wetting the saucer-size
daisies and poppies on her skirt.

At other times (increasingly often lately) I
want to walk up and shove her, making her spill
the juice all over her sweaty neck and her stupid
flowery dress.

Instead, I rise from my chair, dump the bowl
into the sink, and leave the kitchen.

A BOYFRIEND had been prescribed by a psychologist we consulted after my father's first few
months on the couch.

"There is a pattern," Aunt Masha told my mother shortly before that. "They lose their jobs, then they take to spending their days on the couch, and then a woman turns up. *How? When?* you ask yourself. He barely even left the couch!"

It was my uncle Boris who'd first suggested the idea of emigrating. "A scientist of Mikhail's stature will never be properly appreciated in Russia," he said.

I wanted to ask if Cousin Violetta had learned how to ski. The last I heard about her was that she had moved to Aspen and was living with a ski instructor. "The snow in Aspen is as soft as a feather bed and as sweet as cotton candy," she wrote me once. She hadn't written or answered my calls since then.

YOUR HUSBAND and father can't handle the pressure," the psychologist explained. He spoke to my mother and me because my father had stormed out of his office, refusing to be *treated like a madman.*

"He yearns to be relieved, but in a subtle, not humiliating, way. It usually works better if he is relieved by a male child, but sometimes it helps when a daughter marries, thus finding a man who will figuratively replace her father."

The idea filled my mother with almost

religious fervor. "When Tanya finds a boyfriend," she would start frequently, often out of nowhere. "When Tanya finds a boyfriend" signified a wonderful future, when all wishes would come true and all problems dissolve before they even developed. Not only would the boyfriend "relieve" my father, he would also explain to us all the mysterious letters we got from banks, doctors, and gas and electric companies. He would help us move to a bigger, nicer place. "Closer to a subway stop. On the other hand, no. It's too noisy if you live near the subway." The boyfriend, who would of course own a quiet, roomy car like the one we used to have in Russia, would take us upstate to pick mushrooms and blueberries. "Do you think he'll like my mushroom dumplings?" my mother would ask, seeing a shadow of concern on my face.

The only problem was that the wonderful future refused to come.

By the end of our first year in America I'd met only four men who were willing to date me—one at school, the others on the subway—none of them Russian, and none of them even remotely close to the idea of an omnipotent boyfriend. I'd slept with one of them, an Armenian dancer with lips the color of plums and equally firm and smooth. I didn't mention that to my mother.

Around June 1, my mother fished her notebook out of the drawer and planted herself by the telephone. She'd decided to take the business into her own hands.

THE PHONE CALLS from potential boyfriends were rare but consistent. Some weird intuition helped me to distinguish them from other calls by the sharp mocking sound the telephone made.

The receiver felt damp and warm, vibrating with the voice of a strange man trapped inside. The voice is wrong—either too squeaky, too nasal, or too coarse. It is the voice of a man who doesn't want me, who called me because he wanted somebody, anybody—though not me—or simply because his mother made him do it.

Later, on the date, the man casually looked at his toes, but at the same time he discreetly scrutinized me, estimating the size of my breasts, the shape of the legs concealed by my slacks, trying to guess what I would and wouldn't do, trying to guess what was wrong with me (I'd agreed to a blind date, there must be something wrong), searching for flaws, finding them, finding the ones I'd been afraid that he'd find, finding ones I hadn't even known about.

"What is your car's make?" I asked him repeatedly, because I couldn't think of anything else to say.

It's not true that I was not trying, as my mother said. I was trying. I arched my back, I tossed my hair, I licked my lips and crossed my legs in a modest yet seducing way. I nodded sympathetically when he talked, I laughed when he told a joke, I smiled when his shoulders brushed against mine. It didn't help. From the very beginning I knew that eventually I'd fail. Sooner or later the disgust, the humiliation would erupt, and I would end up saying something insulting or indecent, or simply laughing like crazy, kicking with my knees and wiping the tears from my eyes, as I did when my date burped during our dinner.

"You think you're something, don't you?" he had hissed, before adding that he'd never ever ask me out again. "You think you're something!"

I wish I thought that.

AND THEN, all of a sudden, I found a boyfriend. By myself. On a subway train.

It happened on a rainy day at the end of October. A man squeezed into the crowded subway car and brushed against my shoulder with his wet umbrella. I shivered. He said, "Excuse me," walked across the car to the opposite door, and pulled a book out of his shoulder bag.

His clothes were baggy and poorly matched. He looked about six foot two, with a broad body that swayed awkwardly when the train was moving. He kept looking at me from above his book. He liked me for no apparent reason.

After 23rd Street, he stepped forward and grasped a handle above my head. "Do you speak Russian?" he asked.

I said that I did.

He smiled.

That was it.

IT'S DECEMBER and it's snowing outside. I open the door, shaking specks of snow off my knitted hat. He is here. There are his heavy boots, drying on the newspaper in the corner. He visits often. Sometimes he comes before me, sometimes he even comes while I'm at work, and then it's not his shoes but only his wet dark-brown footprints that mark the newspaper on the floor.

"Vadim apologized that he didn't wait for you. He had some errands," my mother yells from the kitchen. Not only has Vadim acquired his own mug and his own chair, there is Vadim's place at the table (by the refrigerator).

The psychologist's prescription has worked. My father's constant lying position became a sitting one—sitting at the computer, after Vadim introduced him to the Internet. He is sending e-mails to mathematicians all over the world, exchanging problems, questions, and even some obscure mathematician jokes.

It is his slouched back that I see now upon coming home. "I've got thirteen e-mails today!" he announces, half turning from his desk and pushing up his glasses. He reads and welcomes everything that comes to his mailbox, from breast-enlargement ads to tax-deduction advice.

"Marochka (Verochka/Genechka), guess who this is?" my mother sings into the receiver every night. She methodically repeats the calling circle of the previous months, making sure she doesn't miss any woman she had begged to find a boyfriend for me.

"By the way, did I mention our Tanya's new boyfriend? . . . Yes, he is Russian. . . . A computer programmer. He's not a Bill Gates, but he is very talented. And nice too. Very nice."

Sometimes he slips and calls my parents Ma and Pa.

"Vadim misses his parents," my mother notes approvingly. His parents had to stay in Moscow because of Vadim's grandfather, who's been bedridden for years. Vadim sends them money, adult diapers for his grandfather, and sugar-free candies for his diabetic grandmother. I know this not from Vadim but from my mother's phone conversations.

"We're pleased. We have nothing to complain about," my mother tells her friends.

I have nothing to complain about either. Even the sex is good—ample and satisfying, like a hearty dinner.

I don't know why seeing Vadim's shoes in the corner makes me recoil.


ANIMATED VOICES invade the apartment. My father's laughter, my mother's murmur, and Vadim's soft baritone buzz against a background of rhythmic knocking and banging. Have they got together to play New Age music?

I make a few steps toward the kitchen and stop, half hidden, in the niche.

They sit at the table with knives and cutting boards around the crystal bowl. They are making Salad Olivier.

"No, Pa, I'm afraid you're wrong." Vadim says. "It's a different salad in *A Moveable Feast*, not Olivier."

"You see! You see!" my mother charges. "What I've been telling you! Olivier can't possibly be without meat."

"Okay, but I still insist that Olivier's name was Jacques."

They take turns emptying their cutting

boards into the bowl, then the rhythmic knocking resumes. The mechanism is working. They don't need me. I am free to go.

I tiptoe out of the kitchen and put on my hat, still wet from the snow. The door opens with a screech; I wait a few seconds to make sure that nobody heard me. A peal of laughter reaches me from the kitchen. I throw a parting look at the warped headline under Vadim's shoes: GOOD NEWS FOR THE DIASPORA!

The snow-covered street is cold and soft. I slowly take it in, the powdered cars, the timid light of the lampposts, the naked twigs of the cherry trees. The weak and helpless snow melts on contact with my feet. It doesn't crunch the way it did in Russia.

I shiver as the cold gets to my toes.

Without me their perfectly tuned mechanism will stop. The gears will slow down and halt. The elements will fall apart.

They need me after all, if only as a link holding them together. I take a handful of the soft feeble snow and knead it in my palms. It melts before I am able to form a shape.

I'M HERE," I say, on entering the kitchen. I walk to the table, push my chair closer, and pick up an egg.

# Luda and Milena

$M$ILENA HAD LARGE BLUE EYES, an elegant nose, and smooth olive skin covered with a graceful network of fine wrinkles. "Her face is a battlefield for antiaging creams," Luda said about Milena, and added that she wouldn't want youth that came from bottles and jars. Once, Luda brought her old photographs to show that she used to be a real beauty too. The photographs revealed an attractive woman with a sturdy hourglass figure, imposing dense brows, and bright, very dark eyes. Some people saw a striking resemblance to the young Elizabeth Taylor, but Milena didn't. Milena said that the young Luda looked like Saddam Hussein with bigger hair and a thinner mustache.

The two women met on the first day of the free ESL class held in one of the musty back rooms of Brooklyn College. Luda was late that day. She had been babysitting her two grandchildren, and her son-in-law had failed to come home on time. Angry and flustered, Luda had to run all the way to Brooklyn College, pushing through the rush-hour subway crowd and cutting across the meat market on Nostrand Avenue, which led to the following exchange with a large woman in a pink jacket:

"Watch it, asshole!" (the woman).

"No, it is you asshole!" (Luda).

By the time Luda opened the classroom door, they had already started the introductions. "My wife and I love America; we want to show it our respect by learning to speak its language," a short man with a shiny nose and shinier forehead was telling the class. A young woman nodded enthusiastically as he spoke. Luda guessed that she must be the teacher. *Angela Waters–Angie–endji* was written on the board. Luda headed toward the wall and the only empty seat, squeezing her large body between the flimsy chairs that sagged under the weight of ESL students. "I'm sorry. . . . Excuse me," she said, when she brushed against somebody with the stretched-out flaps of her cardigan.

"I apologize," she whispered to the thin, elegantly dressed older woman in the next seat. "Don't worry," the woman whispered back in Russian. "Actually, I was afraid they would sit some country bumpkin next to me."

## Luda and Milena

Luda was about to answer with a sympathetic smile, but the smile died in midair. Had her seatmate just expressed relief or confirmation of her fears? She couldn't possibly take her, Ludmila Benina, for a country bumpkin, could she? *You old bitch!* Luda thought, just in case.

She introduced herself in rough but confident English when Angie pointed at her with her chin. "Ludmila Benina, Luda, seventy-two years old, been in the U.S. for four years. I came to this class to improve my grammar and communication skills. I am a widow, I have a daughter and two grandchildren. I used to be a professor of economics in Moscow. I have written three college textbooks. One of my articles was translated into Hindi and appeared in a magazine in India. I used to participate in conferences all over the Soviet Union, and once in Bulgaria." She threw a side glance at her seatmate, to see if she was duly impressed. If she was, her expression didn't betray it.

"Milena from St. Petersburg," she said, when her turn came. Just that. Nothing else. Luda felt stupid. She wished she hadn't brought up the conferences. It would have been enough just to tell about her professorship and her books. She could always have mentioned the conferences later, in future classes, in a casual way. Her unease lasted all through the introductions of two elderly Russian couples; two elderly Chinese couples; three middle-aged Dominican couples; one young and handsome Haitian man; one very tall, very old, and very loud Haitian woman with a funny name, Oolna; and one dark-skinned woman who spoke so fast and with such a heavy accent that nobody could understand what she said or where she came from.

Then a man who sat alone in the back stood up and cleared his throat. "Aron Skolnik, seventy-nine. I used to live in Brooklyn with my wife. She died four years ago. Now I live in Brooklyn alone." Luda raised her eyes and peered at Aron. The expression on his face was strange, uncertain, as if he wasn't sure whether living alone was a bad or a good thing, as if he both welcomed the solitude and found it stifling. Luda had a sudden urge to reach over and touch the thin wisp of hair that stuck to his forehead. And Milena thought she saw a flicker of hunger in Aron's eyes. Just a flicker, but she couldn't be mistaken. He had nice eyes, she decided, the eyes of a much younger man. She straightened her shoulders, removed her Versace shades, shook her hair, and put the shades back on top of her head. Luda snorted and thought, *Look at the old slut!*

.  .  .

## Luda and Milena

THAT NIGHT, as she lay in bed on her stone-hard mattress, Luda continued to think about Milena. There had been this moment, when Luda took off her cardigan and hung it over the chair, that Milena actually sniffed the air and moved deeper into her seat. It was true that Luda hadn't showered in a while, but this was not because she was lazy or had a dislike of cleanliness; it was simply because she had a dislike of cold. She had always preferred hot baths to cold showers, but after being submerged in water that was warmer than air, it felt unbearable to get out. Freezing. Freezing. Trembling. Groping for a towel. Shaking. For some reason cold always filled her with panic. If only there was a way not to become cold afterward, she wouldn't have minded taking a bath. Really. If, for example, there were somebody waiting for her with a large thick towel stretched in his arms. . . . She had a fleeting image of Aron standing in her bathroom, wearing his silly shorts. The image was both touching and ridiculous at the same time.

Luda groaned as she turned onto her side. "It's Sealy orthopedic mattress, Mother, very expensive," Luda's daughter had said. She gave it to Luda after her husband had tried it and hated it. Luda's apartment was almost entirely furnished by her daughter. There was a rickety kitchen table that Luda's daughter had used when she first came to America. There was a flowery sofa that Luda's daughter's friends found too tacky. There was a black bookcase that appeared in Luda's apartment after her daughter had bought a set of light-brown furniture. Only one thing was Luda's own acquisition—a leather armchair with scratched legs and a big cut on the back. Luda had found it standing by a pile of garbage about six blocks away from her home. She called a taxi and paid a driver five dollars for delivery and another five to drag the huge thing upstairs. When they made it to her apartment, Luda felt happy and generous, so she added two more dollars and half of an Entenmann's apple pie as a tip. The armchair had been Luda's prized possession ever since. She especially enjoyed the low groan the armchair made when she sat down. It was the groan of somebody who was profoundly annoyed with Luda but still loved her very much.

MILENA'S APARTMENT was barely furnished at all. She slept on a narrow sofa that she had bought from her brother for sixty dollars. Her TV stood on the floor, and her video player was placed on top of it, which was wrong because it caused the VCR to overheat, as Milena's brother repeatedly pointed out. He had sold her his VCR after he bought a new DVD/VHS player for himself, and he felt it was his duty to ensure that the VCR would be used right. Milena ignored his warning, as she ignored his offer to sell her a large chest of drawers. Her favorite pieces of furniture were her chairs, all nine of them, all different, all bought at one or another garage sale, the price ranging from eight dollars to fifty cents (that one didn't have a seat). She used eight of her chairs as stands for her large photographs and posters, as shelves for vases, and sometimes as hangers for her dresses, because the sight of good clothes never failed to cheer her up. The ninth chair served as a nightstand. It was a wooden chair with a square seat, a perfect size and shape to hold a couple of books and a large shoebox, where she kept her pills, some squeezed-out tubes of expensive antiwrinkle cream, some of her old photographs, and a pencil sketch of the man who had been her lover for over twenty years— including several breakups, other lovers, his never-ending marriage to another woman, and her short-lived marriage to another man.

Milena opened the shoebox and started looking for her sleeping pills, wondering if Luda really used to be as famous and successful as she said. There were so many people who lied. That old Haitian hag in class said she owned a chain of expensive boutiques. A chain! Or that pathetic little man who claimed that he used to be the most famous psychiatrist in Minsk—"You won't believe the bribes they were willing to give just to get an appointment." But Milena didn't really blame them for lying. Actually, when the teacher asked them to introduce themselves, Milena was tempted to lie too. Other people's introductions made her whole life seem like a mocking string of *none*s, *never*s, *no*s, and *so-so*s. She didn't have a husband. She didn't have any children. She'd graduated from a mediocre college. She had worked at the same boring job for thirty years. Once they had offered her a very promising position in Moscow, but she wouldn't leave St. Petersburg, because her lover was in St. Petersburg, and because Moscow was known for being populated by pushy, conceited, obnoxious people. Just look at Luda, with her conferences in Bulgaria!

And then Milena remembered that she had lied in class after all. Her documents stated that her first name was Ludmila. It was her lover who had come up with Milena, claiming that her real name didn't suit her. He saw a Ludmila as a tall languid woman with a thick braid dangling down her spine, and both Luda and Mila, the name's usual diminutives, were too common for her. *Milena* sounded just right. An exotic name, light, nimble, and unique. She used to enjoy that name. She used to enjoy being a small, elegant, irritating puzzle. Now she was too tired to enjoy it. Now she wished she could slump in somebody's arms—to be easy and reachable and to be stroked on the head with tenderness and pity.

THE INTERNATIONAL FEAST, Angie wrote on the white board the next day. "We're going to start this Friday, and then we will have it every week." She had a large blue marker stain on her cheek, but this didn't prevent her from looking enthusiastic. "We'll create a wonderful informal atmosphere, so you all can improve your conversational skills and get acquainted with your diverse cultures. You don't have to bring expensive or complicated dishes, just something simple, something typical of your country." Luda wrote it down: *Fris, feast. Bring Rus. food. Diversity. Culture. Simple.* She looked over Milena's shoulder and saw that Milena had put a fat red star over Friday in her calendar. Of course, Luda thought. An International Feast with all its food, culture, and informal atmosphere was a perfect opportunity to get a man to notice you, and Milena knew this as well as Luda.

On Friday, they pushed some of the desks to the wall to create a makeshift informal space, and put the foil, plastic, and paper containers with food on the teacher's desk in the center. The diverse cultures were represented by fried plantains, duck gizzards, pastelitos, tostones, corn fritters, shrimp spring rolls, two kinds of Russian potato salad, a pack of hard, ring-shaped Russian pretzels, and an extra-value meal from McDonald's brought by the couple who wanted to show their respect to the United States by learning its language. "Our country is America now, we eat American food," the man explained, with the same proud expression. But Angie wouldn't allow her students to start eating. "Mingle, guys, mingle, you have to mingle first," she kept saying. So they all crowded around the desk, sipping soda from plastic cups, trying to ignore the food and make conversation.

Luda studied the room, trying to think of a way to approach Aron through mingling. She was wearing a bright scarf pinched a day before from her daughter's drawer and dark lipstick found at the bottom of the same drawer. "Wipe it off, Grandma," her six-year-old granddaughter had said. "You look stupid." She was afraid that her granddaughter might have been right. Another thing that made Luda uneasy was that she couldn't figure out how to mingle with her classmates. The two Chinese couples wouldn't mingle with anybody but themselves, Dominicans clearly preferred other Dominicans, and the two Russian couples stuck together, with the wives expressing visible displeasure whenever Luda tried to approach them. She had experienced this kind of displeasure before. Her very presence seemed to irk married women of her age, and this was not because they saw her as a threat but rather because her widowhood and loneliness reminded them that they could soon end up like that too. They looked at Luda with wary squeamishness as if she were a scabby dog. Oolna was the only person who didn't mind talking to Luda, but she was too old, and Luda didn't want to appear old by association. As for Aron, he clearly preferred the company of Jean-Baptiste, the handsome young Haitian, seeing kinship in the fact that they were the only two single guys in class. "So tell me, Jean-Baptiste," Aron asked. "Do they try to fix you up? They try to fix me up a lot. But I don't know, I don't know. You know what they say, marry a dancer when you're in your twenties, a masseuse when you're in your forties, and a nurse when you're in your sixties. But what about me, my friend? I'm seventy-nine." Luda sighed. There was no way she could break into this conversation.

Milena wasn't mingling either. She had flitted in like a summer breeze, put a pack of square Russian biscuits on the table, and sat down on the edge of one of the desks, not looking at anybody, one leg over the other. Summer breeze with creaking joints, Luda thought, but she was worried. One passing look from Milena told her that she did appear stupid in her scarf and her caked lipstick. Luda knew that look very well. Mocking, condescending, sometimes pitying. She had seen it all too often on the faces of her husband's countless secretaries, all attractive single women.

Milena smoothed the folds on her skirt and looked out the window. She thought she'd just sit and wait until Aron noticed her. "Impress and ignore" had been her strategy for years, but she wasn't sure if it still worked. It had been awhile since she'd lost her ability to turn heads, and sometimes she thought that the saddest thing about it was that she couldn't say exactly when it had happened. Men used to look at her, and then they didn't. Something used to be there, and then it was gone; it was as if a part of her died and she hadn't even noticed when. Still, Milena couldn't think of any other strategy. She knew that trying to approach other couples was pointless— married women of her age looked at her as if she were a disease. Their warning stares reminded her of the expression on the face of her lover's wife in the photograph he kept on his desk. Every time Milena happened to see it, she felt that the wife was staring directly at her, at times begging her to leave her husband alone, at other times threatening. Luda looked a little like her. The same heavy features, the same stupid scarf. Respectable, boring, the very picture of righteousness.

Oh, really? Luda thought to herself, having caught Milena's stare. Respectable? Boring? For your information, I have had lovers too. *Lovers* was stretching it a bit, but Luda had had one encounter, with a colleague, on the last night of the three-day conference in Bulgaria. The man's name was Stoyan; he was heavy and dark, with jet black hair spurting above his collarbone. He offered to see her to her hotel, and as they walked, discussing the problems of the advanced Socialist economic system, Luda couldn't help but marvel at the linguistic similarity of his name to the Russian word for *erection*. Later, in bed, he had wanted her to yell out his name, but she wouldn't; she was too bashful for that. I'm not as innocent as you think, Luda thought, fixing her scarf with defiance. Let's just see.

But then Angie announced that it was time to eat, and the students ditched their conversation partners and rushed toward the food. Plastic tops covering the dishes were removed, foil was peeled off, paper containers unclasped, and the room filled with happy clatter and the air with culturally diverse aromas of curry, ginger, garlic, and basil. The spring rolls were the first to go. It seemed as if one moment there was a whole plateful of them, and the next there was nothing but the oily stains on the students' fingers and a wonderful shrimp-and-scallions aftertaste in their mouths. Tostones and pastelitos followed suit. The Dominicans and the Russians were a little skeptical about duck gizzards but soon learned to appreciate them. Nobody was particularly enthusiastic about the two varieties of potato salad, so the two Russian couples who brought them ate each other's offerings. And the extra-value-meal couple ate their extra-value meal. By the end of the feast there were only two items left, the hard, round pretzels and the hard, square biscuits. Angie ate one of each and politely pronounced them authentic and interesting, but nobody else appeared to share her interest.

Both Luda and Milena saw they'd made a mistake: they should have brought something more exciting. They knew it as soon as they saw how Aron's face changed when the food was uncovered. At first his expression was hopeful but uncertain, as if he were a child seeing his favorite toy but wasn't sure if it was meant for him or not. But as he filled his plate, his cautious grin disappeared in the deep furrows of a beaming smile. He chewed slowly, with his eyes closed, making sounds similar to the drone of a happy electric appliance. His cheeks became flushed and tiny beads of sweat gathered on the bridge of his nose.

"Who made this? This is divine!" he would exclaim from time to time. Aron finished the last spring roll, crinkled his nose, and laughed. He looked radiant; he looked twenty years younger; he looked—Luda couldn't think of a word right away, and then it hit her—he looked inspired. You couldn't help but smile when watching Aron eat. And so Luda smiled. And Milena smiled too. Luda and Milena had heard that the path to a man's heart ran through his stomach, but they'd never believed it. Aron Skolnik proved them wrong.

THE PROBLEM was that neither Luda nor Milena cooked. Milena had a particularly tortured relationship with food. For years and years, her life had been structured around her lover's visits. He would come to her place after work, twice a week, to spend about an hour with her. "No, no," he would say, when she offered him food. "Let's not waste time. My wife is waiting for me with dinner anyway." Milena would attempt to cook for herself at times, out of spite, out of defiance. She would mix the ingredients in the bowl, telling herself that she didn't care; she would cook and enjoy a good meal by herself. "I don't care, I don't care," she would still be saying as she scooped the contents of the bowl into the garbage pail.

And Luda? Luda had always been too busy working. Moreover, for most of her married life she had lived with her mother-in-law, who cooked a lot and enjoyed cooking, especially if she could come up with a dish that Luda couldn't stand. Once Luda figured that out, she learned to fake her culinary partialities. To confuse her mother-in-law, she would feign great enthusiasm for the food she hated ("Zucchini pancakes! Can I have another helping?") and appear indifferent to something she really liked. She mastered the art of faking so well that by the time her mother-in-law died and Luda could finally start eating according to her real partialities, she found that she no longer had partialities. Her sense of taste was ruined, her interest in food gone.

Which didn't mean that she couldn't learn how to cook, Luda thought, on the Thursday before the next feast, while flipping TV channels at home. Learning how to cook was a challenge, and she was used to meeting challenges head on. The first three shows of Food Network were a complete waste. Luda couldn't care less about the chili cookoff, nor did she need information about candy-making technology. In the third show, the host explained how to make tiramisu, which could have been helpful if not for her cleavage—so prominent that Luda couldn't concentrate on the movements of the woman's hands. The fourth show, however, turned out to be much better. The host was making Greek feta and spinach pie, and she seemed to know what she was doing. Besides, the cleavage, if there was any, was well hidden under her chef's jacket. Luda opened her brand-new notebook and prepared to write down the instructions.

The pie did work! Luda herself was surprised how well it worked. She had had some doubts as she was spreading the filling over the dough. To make the pie more authentically Russian, she had substituted cabbage for spinach, boiled eggs for feta cheese, and gotten rid of pine nuts altogether. She had a moment of worry that maybe those stupid pine nuts were the key ingredient after all. But when Luda took the pie out, not as perfect as on TV, far from perfect, but warm, and gleaming, and fragrant, all her doubts disappeared. She knew it would work. She closed her eyes and imagined that her own pie looked just as golden and perfect, and then she imagined Aron's smile, and then—and this was the most delicious image—the stunned and furious expression on Milena's face.

ARON ACTUALLY MOANED when he tried the first piece. When he finished the second piece, he took a napkin, wiped his lips, and looked at Luda.

Looked at her and saw her. It had been such a long time since men saw her when they looked at her. "So good. I could eat it every day and not get tired of it," he said. But even this didn't give her as much thrill as the lost expression on Milena's face. Poor Milena, Luda thought. Poor Milena, who wore a low-cut blouse and had brought store-bought eggplant caviar and to whom Aron said, "Did you buy it at the International on 5th and Brighton? They make a much better one in the Taste of Europe in Bensonhurst." Poor, poor Milena.

I WONDER what the fat pig will make today, Milena thought, as she entered the bathroom the next Friday morning with a steaming coffee mug, a pack of cigarettes, and a book squeezed under her arm. Milena sat down on the toilet, put her coffee and the book on top of the laundry hamper, and lit a cigarette. People like Luda resembled battering rams; they would pummel and pummel, patiently, without taking a break, for as long as it took them to get what they wanted. Her lover's wife was the same way, and she got her prize in the end; she still had her husband, who finally became a really good husband, because by now he was too old, too worn out, too scared, and too beaten to cheat. And Milena, stupid proud Milena, who had always thought it was beneath her to fight for a man, what did she gain? Nothing. She wound up with nothing. Just look at her: old and alone, sitting on a toilet with a coffee mug and a cigarette! Well, she wasn't above fighting for a man this time.

She took a sip of coffee and started leafing through her book—*pozharskie kotlety, kotlety po-kievski, rasstegai*—an old cookbook, with fine yellowed pages and elaborate drawings, a legacy from Milena's allegedly aristocratic grandmother. There were countless long mornings when Milena's grandmother would sit little Milena at the table and teach her how to make *pozharskie kotlety* or *rasstegai*. Afterward, she graded Milena's work, usually poorly, because Milena was too impatient and wouldn't do everything just so. How she hated those mornings! But she had learned how to cook. Surprise, surprise, fat pig!

LOOK, GUYS, we have something new from one of our Russian students today," Angie said, taking a blue cotton napkin off Milena's porcelain plate. There under a napkin were perfect golden squares of cheese puffs that smelled as if they had been taken out of the oven a second ago. There was a secret to that, which Milena's grandmother had shared with Milena as a gift on her sixteenth birthday (Milena would have preferred new earrings). The puffs were so beautiful that people couldn't bring themselves to grab them, as they did with other food at the feast. They picked up pieces with two fingers and chewed slowly and didn't talk while they chewed, so all you could hear were the sounds of small crunchy bites. When all the puffs were gone, Aron flicked the few golden crumbs off his shirt and asked Milena what her name was. "Beautiful and unusual," he commented.

Luda didn't know much about medicine, so she didn't know if extreme frustration and anger could cause an immediate heart attack. She decided that they couldn't, because if they could she would be dead by now. The worst thing was the look on Milena's face when Luda unpeeled the foil cover on her offering. The bitch actually chuckled. Yes, Luda had brought another Greek/ Russian cabbage pie. So what? It worked the last time; what was so stupid about assuming that it would work again? Luda loosened her scarf and sat down, hoping that either she or all the other students, along with Aron and Milena, would disappear somehow. She tried telling herself that Milena's offering wasn't better, it was simply new, but this thought failed to console her, as it had failed to console her many years ago, every time she sniffed yet another scent of a new perfume on her husband's shirt.

The big heavy arm on her shoulder made Luda flinch. "I didn't like her puffs," Oolna said. "Show off. Not real food." Luda wanted to bury her face in Oolna's soft, boundless chest and cry with gratitude. And then the wife from one of the Russian couples sidled in and whispered that she didn't like the puffs either. "Too salty, didn't you think? And she is wearing way too much makeup for her age." Luda smiled and happily shared her observation that Milena's face looked like a battlefield for antiaging creams.

IN THE WEEKS to come, Luda saw that she wasn't just an annoying old woman anymore, she was the star of the show. The whole net of clumsy alliances was quickly spinning around her. There was Oolna, the oldest and truest of her fans. There was the Russian wife, and there was the Dominican couple who didn't like feeling intimidated by Milena's clothes and demeanor. The husband even made a show out of mocking Milena's haughty manner of walking into the room, and the members of Luda's fan club eagerly laughed.

But Milena too found herself surrounded by allies. First of all, there was the Chinese woman who had nursed a grudge against Luda since the day when Luda's pie managed to outshine her spring rolls. Her other ally was the wife from the second Russian couple, who identified herself (somewhat incorrectly) with elegant, sophisticated women like Milena. And there was the second Chinese couple, who joined the camp simply because they always sided with the first Chinese couple. All of them laughed happily when Milena compared Luda to Saddam Hussein. The husband of the second Chinese couple was deaf in one ear, so his wife had to retell him the joke loudly and in Chinese, and then he laughed too.

But while both camps acknowledged that there was a contest going on, and while everybody knew what the main prize was, nobody ever mentioned Aron. They couldn't help but wonder, though, whether he knew what the competition was all about. If he knew, he never showed it. He seemed to be bent on preserving his independence and his right to favor the winner. There were Fridays when Luda's dish would come out too sloppy (either the fault of one or another Food Network host or of Luda's overt zeal). And there were Fridays when Milena's offering would be just a bit too subtle or too bland. And since Aron's romantic gestures always went strictly in sync with the competition, Luda's and Milena's gains and losses in intimacy were fluctuating as well. There were Fridays when Aron seemed to have formed a special connection with Luda. He would sit and talk with her in the corner (after the best food was gone, never before), he would joke with her, he would ask her about her life and even make vague plans for the future, something like, "Do you like Manhattan Beach? It's nice down there. I go for a stroll sometimes. Not too often." And sometimes he would even walk her home. Once Aron kissed Luda on the cheek. His lips felt warm and dry and vaguely disappointing.

And there were Fridays that belonged to Milena. Aron would walk Milena home and try to brush against her sleeve or touch the flaps of her jacket, and once he attempted to play with her necklace. Sometimes he would even share his memories. One time, for example, he told her about a lovely woman with whom he had had a brief but passionate affair and who looked just like Milena, "No, seriously, the same eyes, the same cheekbones, even the same oval mole on the neck."

But just as it happened with Luda, Aron never walked Milena all the way to her house. He would stop a few blocks away from her building and say that walking was getting harder and harder; he'd better head back. And just as it happened with Luda, come Monday, all the Friday intimacy was gone. He never gave any sign that they had formed some kind of connection, never spoke to either of them before or after class, hardly even looked at them. On Mondays, there was no indication that he wanted either of them, or that he ever would. On Mondays, Luda and Milena felt deflated and tired too, and perhaps even a little ashamed of their Friday excitement. But as the week was coming to an end, the memories of Aron at his best (or perhaps fantasies of what Aron could have been like at his best) grew more and more intense. Luda imagined how she would stroll with Aron on Manhattan Beach past all the other couples, and how if her daughter ever tried to push another piece of furniture on her, she would refuse, saying that her husband didn't like it. And Milena thought of being in bed with Aron and how he would smile at her and tell her that she still had it. And as Luda's and Milena's fantasies flourished, so did their fear and fury at the thought that he could pick the other as the ultimate winner.


THE AFTERNOON before the last International Feast, Luda plugged in the food processor, pushed cubes of beef and lamb down the tube, and pressed the button. The mere image of Aron leaving with Milena after the last International Feast (with Milena's allies rejoicing and Luda's allies saying something unconvincing about Aron's unsubstantial worth as a boyfriend) would send Luda into a state of murderous rage. For several weeks now, all her thoughts were concentrated on her final dish.

The food processor, another discard from her daughter's pantry, was an old bulky thing with a crack on the side covered by a piece of duct tape. It whirred and vibrated and jumped all over the table surface, but it did its job well. Luda smiled as she watched how the meat cubes bounced under the knives. The onion got stuck in the tube, and she had to hit it with the wooden spoon handle to push it down. Luda stopped before reaching for a bowl where the bread had been soaking in milk; she wasn't sure if the bread had to go into the food processor or not.

MILENA MOVED about her kitchen quickly and gracefully. She prodded the bread with her finger to check if it was soggy enough. She knew that when making meatballs you should never put the bread into a food processor. First of all, the bread was soft and soggy enough to be easily broken with a fork, but—most important—coarsely minced bread was essential for making meatballs fluffy and plump. She put the bread into the bowl with the ground veal, added some crushed garlic (a lot of it) and a couple of eggs, and started working the mix with the fork, enjoying the slurping sound.

AND NOW for the secret ingredient," Luda thought, throwing small cubes of pancetta into the hissing skillet. "Pancetta," The Food Network host had moaned, "So good, your guests won't know what hit them!"

FAT, MILENA THOUGHT, all the flavor was in the fat, and people are just kidding themselves when they try to believe otherwise. She put a chunk of nice sweet butter and a smaller chunk of lard in the middle of the skillet and swirled it around. The rest was easy.

NO, THIS WASN'T hard at all, Luda decided. Especially if you found the perfect method. She shaped the balls and threw them onto the hissing skillet with her right hand while holding the spatula with her left. When the meat under her fingers got all warm and sticky, she rinsed her right hand under cold running water and started again. Her small kitchen was quickly filling with smoke and the smell of burning fat, but Luda didn't pay any attention to that. She worked very fast. So did Milena. It was amazing how fast the bowl was becoming empty. As she was shaping the last meatball, Milena had a sudden urge to squeeze it. And she did just that, so hard that tiny bits of soggy meat came out between her fingers. She wiped her hand and went to open the window.

ON THE MONDAY after the last International Feast, Angie's hands trembled so much she had to grip the wrist of her right hand with her left to be able to write on the board. Her legs trembled as well, so she went to sit down in the low chair that stood by her desk. She said that it would be nice if everybody said a few words about Aron.

One of the Dominicans said that it was too bad that Aron didn't have a family. "That's a wonderful observation," Angie noted.

A man from one of the Chinese couples said that Aron taught everybody a lesson. "This is an excellent point." Angie nodded and reached into her purse for a tissue.

She had never had a student die during her class before. Nobody she knew had ever had a student die during class. She had been plagued by ghastly flashbacks throughout the whole weekend. Bright and loud, the images of the last feast kept spinning in her head as if she were caught inside a horror movie. And now the movie was starting to play again.

They tune the radio to some nasty Latino music. They uncover the food. The smell! She is so sick of that smell. They stomp their feet to the beat of the music. Poor Aron, happy as a child. Moving closer to the table. Filling his plate. Gorging. Starting to choke. They all step away in horror. Angie pushes buttons on her phone. For the life of her she can't remember which buttons to push. Jean-Baptiste rushes forward, grabs Aron from behind; his fist thrusts into Aron's stomach. Thrusts again. Again and again. Finally! The fucking Russian meatball is out! Sighs of relief all over the room. Angie snaps her phone closed. And then Aron's legs go slack and Jean-Baptiste starts to sway under Aron's weight. For a moment it looks like they are dancing together to the loud beats of Latino music. Old Oolna starts to laugh, a horrible cackling laugh. And then, only then, they finally realize what has just happened. . . .

Angie blew her nose and looked over her silent class. "Do you want to say something, Jean-Baptiste?"

"Yeah. Aron was a funny man."

"Good, Jean-Baptiste, good," Angie agreed.

Luda said that they would all miss Aron, and

Milena said that his was an enviable death. Angie raised her brows at her.

"Quick and easy. And he died happy, didn't he?" Milena explained in a calm patient voice.

Angie shuddered and pronounced the class over.

It was cold and very bright outside. Milena reached into her bag for her sunglasses, but Luda only squinted her eyes.

"Going down that way?" Milena asked. Luda nodded. They started walking down the street together.

"You know," Luda said, after a while, "I don't enjoy cooking that much."

"Me neither," Milena said, and they continued to walk.

# Slicing Sautéed Spinach

*F*OR ALMOST A YEAR, Ružena had been eating spinach in restaurants. She'd eaten sautéed spinach in Italian eateries, creamed spinach in old-fashioned American diners, pureed spinach in Indian places, and once she even ate spinach dumplings in a dark and overheated Mongolian restaurant on East 12th Street. Ružena didn't have any particular fondness for spinach; she ate it simply because her lover ordered it for her. "It's easy," he would say, urging her to order. "You pick what you want to eat and you say it aloud."

But it wasn't easy for Ružena. She felt apprehensive when a menu appeared before her, panicky when she opened it, and paralyzed with fear when she read the fine script describing what was served on a bed of what and under which sauce. So many choices! So easy to make an embarrassing one! Ružena begged her lover to order something for her, anything, the same thing he wanted to eat. He agreed. And since his gastronomic preferences were limited to salmon, rice, and spinach, those three things invariably appeared on Ružena's plate. Nothing could tempt Ružena to eat salmon (she was allergic to fish) or rice (she simply hated it), so she ended up eating only spinach. Ružena didn't dislike spinach. She would even have said that she didn't mind spinach, if it weren't so difficult to slice.

On their first date they ate sautéed spinach with garlic and pine nuts in a red-brick Italian place. On the walls, black-and-white photographs glistened in candlelight. They had met a few days before on a bench in the Central Library while waiting for their order. The man pointed at the electronic board above their heads. "I can't stand the thing. Reminds me of hours spent in Department of Motor Vehicles lines. The mere sight of those changing numbers stirs up memories of parking tickets, lost licenses, expired inspections. You know, that nagging feeling of driver's guilt."

The man shook his head, making his fine light-brown hair fly off his forehead and land back.

"Don't you hate it?"

Ružena nodded, even though she didn't own a car and wasn't familiar with driver's guilt. She kept peering at the electronic board as if her whole future depended on seeing her number there, not turning to the man, merely answering further questions with nods or one-syllable words. To the question, was she a student in New York? she said *yes*. To the question, where had she come from? she said *Prague*. And to the question, could he call her sometime? she answered with a nod. With her side vision, Ružena caught the vague shape of a tall man in jeans and a tweed jacket. She hoped his books would arrive first and he would leave without seeing hers, books documenting eighteenth-century birth control and female hygiene. Her wish came true and the man left, after putting a crumpled piece of paper with Ružena's number into his jeans pocket.

Later that day, the hazy image of the man appeared to Ružena several times. First, when she sat in a subway car, squeezed between two chatting women whose voices seemed to bounce off the sides of her head. Another time, on the pages of her paper about an eighteenth-century diaphragm and the French prostitute who invented it. The last image appeared late that night, in Ružena's tiny Brooklyn apartment, while she watched the news with her Polish roommate. They were both dressed in sweatpants, T-shirts, and oversized slippers and were munching on baby carrots rather than fattening chips; the man appeared to her on a train going through the countryside. They were sitting across from each other and talking—or, rather, Ružena talked and the man listened. By the time the weather broadcast came on, the train image was replaced with one of Ružena standing by the window with a little boy, vaguely resembling the man, nestled in her arms. The boy giggled and sucked on Ružena's hair. Look, a birdie, she wanted to tell him, but she wasn't sure which language should she use, Czech or English. "Definitely Czech," she decided. "He will pick up English when he is older."

"I'm turning off this crap," her roommate said. She pressed the button and shuffled to her room, struggling to free a piece of carrot stuck in her teeth.

THE CANDLE on their table exuded a faint smell that resembled burning plastic. The flickering light fell on Ružena's plate in a few uneven spots, illuminating the spinach that didn't look like Ružena had expected. The twisted brown strips resembled malnourished earthworms. She attempted to slice off a piece, but the knife made whiny sounds and proved helpless before the rubberlike matter. Ružena was deciding between twisting the strips on a fork, as if it were pasta, or leaving the spinach jumble alone, when she felt the man's hand just above her knee. His words rustled in her hair. "I want to take your clothes off and make love to you."

*What a cliché!* the critical part of Ružena protested. Yet her uncritical part melted just like the plastic-smelling candle on the table. It had been more than a year since a man had touched her knee or whispered to her.

Ružena gulped ice water while comparing the man's description of her beauty with her reflection in the stainless-steel pitcher. She did have an unusual face, with regular if slightly sharp features, dense eyebrows, light-blue eyes, and pale skin that easily blushed and broke into blotches. She wasn't sure if she could be called "breathtakingly beautiful," but she agreed that her flaxen hair looked "spectacular"—she had washed it just before the date and hadn't spared expensive conditioner. As for her "magnificent" Eastern European accent, Ružena could only shrug. She'd always thought of it as an embarrassing handicap, imagining that the English words came out of her mouth either wounded or coated in mud.

"I want to be your lover," the man whispered. He spread his fingers wider on Ružena's thigh, elaborating a long speech in which Ružena caught the word *marriage* close to the end. "I don't take marriage lightly. It's probably not the sanest decision, but I've made it and I'm going to stick to it."

For a second Ružena thought he was proposing

to her. Then she realized he was talking about another woman, his fiancée, with whom he'd been living for almost six years. This man was about to marry someone else, but he wanted to be Ružena's lover.

"I won't push you," he said, by the restaurant door. His fingers were cool as he ran his hand between her shoulder blades.

Ružena's roommate wasn't home that night, so she took the opportunity to eat cream cheese out of the container. Hunched on the kitchen windowsill, Ružena scooped up the cheese with brittle Ritz crackers, while repulsion at the man's offer fought against the stubborn memories of his touch.

If he cheats on his fiancée, it's his moral dilemma, not mine. I should enjoy myself now; I don't care about the future. I'm not interested in marriage. How many people do I know who have benefited from one? Ružena had the whole arsenal of worn-out but sturdy arguments to defeat the repulsion. Still, repulsion probably would have won if only loneliness weren't so exhausting. Loneliness followed her everywhere like an unwelcome companion, creeping in at parties she attended, sitting beside her at matinees in a movie theater, dragging along when she took a walk, staring at her mockingly from the cream-cheese surface littered with cracker crumbs.

She removed all the crumbs with a teaspoon before returning the container to the refrigerator.

ON THEIR second date, she ate old-fashioned creamed spinach in a crowded diner. It didn't taste particularly good, but Ružena swallowed one steaming spoonful after another. They had just made love in his friend's apartment, where the air conditioner had been blowing full blast the whole time. The man took her clothes off and stepped back to savor the sight. Ružena had never felt quite so naked. With her lovers back home, she had gone on dates for weeks, sometimes months, while they gradually revealed and touched all of each other's body parts before going to bed. So when they saw each other fully naked at last, there were no surprises. They had enough time to get used to all the little imperfections and to begin to see each scar, each birthmark, and each stubborn twist of hair as a familiar and endearing attribute of the lover's body.

This time, in front of the stranger, Ružena's whole body shrank, resisting being exposed to judgment, wary of confirming her gender. She covered her breasts with her elbows. She resisted acknowledging that her pale pathetic mess of a body could actually attract a man, was so obviously attracting a man, while her mind begged her body to yield, to behave according to the situation, not to show its fear and embarrassment.

Ružena's spoon clinked against the bottom of her bowl. The man whispered something, but she couldn't make out the words in the diner's noise.

"What?" she asked.

"You were fantastic."

Are you kidding? she almost said, barely managing to keep her mouth from gaping.

"Was it good for you too?"

Ružena put her spoon down. It would have been awfully impolite not to give him a compliment in return. "Yes," she said. "It's been wonderful."

They met once a week, during his lunch hour, at his friend's place on East 18th. Soon everything in the apartment became so familiar to her that she could see the wallpaper pattern—green diamonds and lilac wavy lines—with her eyes closed and name all the titles in the bookcase, starting with the self-help books on the upper shelves and ending with the heavy art volumes on the lower. Their lovemaking usually took just over an hour. Ružena learned to glance up at the antique clock to see when her lover was about to climax. Afterward they went out to lunch, sampling rice and spinach in one or another ethnic restaurant in the neighborhood. They walked separately, so nobody would see them together.

That didn't bother Ružena. His shy request not to tell anyone didn't bother her either. She even liked it in a way. She didn't have a boyfriend, but she had a secret. Her life had become more interesting with a secret: more mysterious, less straightforward. Loneliness, if not disappearing entirely, didn't follow her as closely as before.

ONCE THEY WERE seated at a table, the man smiled at her, made a quick compliment to their lovemaking, ordered their lunch, and began talking. "It feels wonderful to talk to you," he often said.

Ružena had heard that before. She credited it to the fact that she didn't talk much herself.

They talked about his job. He edited a respectable scientific magazine, which required dealing with impossible deadlines, an unpredictable boss, and his pregnant assistant, who broke into sobs whenever he pointed out her mistakes. They talked about his friends and his fiancée, whom he described as if they were television characters, labeled with one or two personality traits and behaving according to them. As they ate their spinach empanadillas, he confided that he was writing a book.

"I've been writing it for over ten years. Actually, it isn't going along well. In fact, I often wake up in the middle of the night overcome with a surge of panic that at forty-five I'm a complete failure."

The spinach empanadillas—tiny puffed pies—would have been very convenient to eat if the stuffing didn't fall out so easily. Ružena didn't know whether she should pick it up and put it back into her mouth or leave it on the plate. She asked what the book was about.

"It's a memoir—well, not exactly a memoir. I would rather call it a novel with a strong presence of me."

Sometimes he asked about Ružena's school—she was pursuing a PhD in Women's Studies—or about her country, which Ružena described in a calm and precise manner, without the ridicule or nostalgia typical of most emigrants.

They were eating spinach gnocchi when he asked, "Do you miss your country at all?"

Ružena swallowed the piece that she had just put in her mouth and was about to answer his question, when she felt a spasm in her throat. A scalding flow of tears coursed down her cheeks. She grabbed the linen napkin off her lap and pressed it to her eyes.

In a few seconds, her banquette sagged under the man's weight. "Tell me," he whispered. "Tell me, what is it?"

Ružena turned away, trying to hide her face

behind the rough fabric of the napkin. She had nothing to tell, nothing that could justify a breakdown in a public place. He'll either think that I'm suffering from a bad case of homesickness or that something horrible happened at home, Ružena thought in panic. For a second, she was tempted to invent a lie. She ran through a jumble of television images in her head, choosing between killing off her mother, her father, or her nonexistent twin sister.

She let the napkin slide down her face. Her lover looked blurry behind the screen of tears, his features distorted as in an abstract painting. He sat too close to her. There wasn't enough space between them, not enough for her to lie.

She told him that she used to miss home very much. She told him that images of Prague, obscure, often false, used to haunt her during her first year in America.

"I would hunt for glimpses of Prague landscapes in New York streets. I would raid Brooklyn groceries in search of strawberries that tasted like the ones at home. I would go to my room at night, slump on a chair at my desk, drop my head on a pile of books, and just give in to longing. There was one place that I especially missed: a tiny bakery, which for some reason always smelled like fresh laundry. You know, the stuffy, hot smell of boiled sheets? I'd never liked that smell, but here in New York I became infatuated by it. I would sniff the air every time I passed a Laundromat, feeling the tingle in my stomach. I was reluctant to visit Prague for a long time, fearing I wouldn't find the strength to go back to New York. But when I went home at last, I felt cheated. I visited all my favorite places, I saw all my friends, I ate all the food I had longed for, but I didn't feel the tingle, not even in the bakery. The smell was still there, but it didn't move me at all. I went back to New York, hoping my homesickness would return—you know, we always wish for something that we can't have. But it didn't. I went home every night and slumped in my chair with nothing to long for."

Ružena dabbed her eyes and nose with the napkin and glanced up at the man apologetically. That was all she had to tell.

The man's eyelashes blinked frequently as if they were operated by some mechanism. He suddenly moved toward her and closed his hands around her back in one startling movement. She felt the hard seam of his jeans on her stockinged calf, the stiff collar of his shirt pressed to her wet neck, the warm, stuffy fabric of his jacket touching her whole body, his breath smelling of Italian spices enveloping her face. She freed her arms and hugged him back.

Afterward they ordered more gnocchi. The

man moved his plate from the other side of the table to sit next to her. He sprinkled freshly grated Parmesan over her plate, refilled her glass, and entertained her with some silly stories of his childhood.

Ružena, suddenly ravenous, ate all of her gnocchi and then some from his plate.

SIX DAYS LATER they ate lunch in an Indian restaurant, where the booths resembled bamboo huts with straw mats for seats. They had been asked to leave their shoes outside the booth, and Ružena felt funny sitting barefoot in a restaurant. She smiled at her lover, who had been unusually silent at his friend's apartment.

They were served bitter spinach puree, too spicy for Ružena. She'd said, "Mild, please," when asked by the waiter, but apparently her voice had been too low. She was licking smidgens of spinach off the tines of her fork when the man spoke at last.

"Ružena," he said.

She'd never noticed how harsh her name sounded in English.

"Ružena, I can't marry you."

The rest poured out in long, emotionally charged sentences. He wanted to be honest with her, he didn't want to give her the wrong idea, his life was not going to change, he couldn't allow their relationship to become too intimate, he couldn't afford to have two women emotionally dependent on him. He was sorry, but he couldn't marry her.

Ružena stared at her six-year-old boots on the floor next to the booth—their drooping tops, scuffed heels, toes scraped raw from a shoe polish brush. For once they weren't hidden under the table but in plain view. She could feel burning spots blooming on her face and neck. Why was it that he assumed she wanted to marry him? Was it because of the breach in her careful detachment the last time, the hazardous leak of affection? Or perhaps there was another, more cynical reason for his assumption: It was natural for her—poor, lonely, and uprooted—to want to marry him—stable, successful, secure. The worst thing was that he might have been right. What if she did want to marry him? What if she did hope he would ditch his fiancée one day and marry her?

"Look, Ružena, I don't want to hurt you. I really like you. I would have wanted very much to continue seeing you, if only we could find the right balance. You see, right now our relationship is out of balance."

Ružena watched spoonfuls of spinach vanish in his roomy mouth while he talked. She'd felt that mouth on hers every week for several months. The wave of repulsion made her dizzy.

"Fuck you and your balance!" she wanted to yell. But instead of cursing his balance, she waited. The man chewed on a piece of naan.

"You don't have to worry about balance. I have a fiancé too. I am sorry I didn't mention him before; the right moment never came up."

Ružena smiled. It was easier than she'd imagined. Her heart pounded, but that didn't worry her. The heart wasn't anything that people could see.

THE NEXT WEEK, over *épinards à la crème*, she told him her fiancé's name was Pavel. They sat opposite each other in a small restaurant with wicker chairs, maps of France on the walls, and rude waitresses who spoke with an accent (Ružena wasn't sure if it was French). The *épinards à la crème*, for some reason, was adorned with a fried egg.

"Pavel?" Her lover pierced the egg yolk with his fork. "*Pavel* is a beautiful name."

Ružena thought so too.

"What does he do?"

Pavel was a physicist. He'd graduated from Prague University and was offered a job in France. (For some reason the combination of physics and France thrilled Ružena.) He lived near Strasbourg, in a village at the crossing of two rivers, the names of which she had forgotten. Ružena was looking at a map behind the man's back.

It didn't take a lot of effort to endow Pavel with a name, a profession, and a place of residence. All she had to do now was to add a few details, which turned out to be easy, even enjoyable.

All the men who used to be unattainable—her girlfriends' boyfriends, college professors, movie actors, movie characters, dead writers, cousins, uncles—were now at her disposal, providing appearance and character traits, lifestyles, habits, even clothing patterns. How many times before had she wished that her boyfriend had one or another wonderful trait he lacked or had been spared the nasty one he possessed? Ružena felt as if the doors of a magic store were opened for her. She could roam between shelves, picking items she liked, refusing others. She chose her cousin Pavel's name, Uncle Milan's smile, her ophthalmologist's beard, the heavy eyelids of her favorite Russian actor, and the aquiline nose of a French one. She selected the loose corduroy pants that her philosophy professor wore, and the plaid shirts favored by her first boyfriend, Zdenek. She spared her fiancé Uncle Milan's schizophrenia, the Russian actor's weak chin, and Zdenek's habit of picking his nose while reading. She could have a man made to order.

*Épinards à la crème* tasted better than most of the spinach dishes she'd tried before. It wasn't overdone, yet it didn't have a grassy taste. She ate several large spoonfuls before answering more questions about Pavel. No, they didn't mind the separation. It had been their choice to lead separate lives for some time before marriage. No, Pavel didn't know about this particular lover, but they both had a realistic concept of "separate lives."

The man had an attentive look on his face. He stopped eating and sat making holes in his spinach with the fork. There were yellow traces of egg yolk around his mouth. "Your Pavel sounds too perfect," he said at last.

"Does he?" Ružena scraped the remains of creamed spinach off the bottom of her bowl. "Well, he is not."

Ružena began granting her fiancé flaws. What started as a way of achieving authenticity soon turned into a source of pleasure. It was the imperfections—the awkward strokes of a paintbrush, tiny dabs of dirt, barely visible scratches on the canvas—that made Pavel lovable. Ružena had to confine herself to granting Pavel only one fault at a time. Over German spinach salad with walnuts and apple bits, Pavel was given a gift of clumsiness. Over Mongolian spinach dumplings, he acquired slightly crooked front teeth. Over yet another dish of sautéed spinach, stubbornness. (By that time Ružena had become proficient at slicing spinach. It wasn't tricky or sophisticated, as she'd thought before. It simply required some practice.)

"Pavel grips the fork in his fist. He pierces his food as if he were a knight with a spear. I laugh at him, but he insists that it's more convenient," Ružena said once, watching the annoyingly elegant movements of her lover's fork. Lately, she had noticed that most of Pavel's favorite imperfections sprang from the things she didn't like about her lover. She was surprised that there were so many of them.

Soon Pavel obtained a real presence at their table. They could almost see him in the extra chair or the corner of the booth, quiet, a little clumsy, wiping pieces of food off his beard with a napkin, his checkered elbow dangerously close to a glass of water or a puddle of sauce on the table.

"Pavel hates spinach," Ružena announced. The waiter had just handed them menus. "He likes vegetables that remain bright when cooked: carrots, peppers, zucchini, asparagus. 'I want my plate to look like a painter's palette,' he says."

She suddenly realized that was exactly what *she* wanted: a plate that looked like a painter's palette, heaped with colorful, crunchy chunks sprinkled with garlic and lemon juice, glistening with butter. She reached for the menu. Somehow it didn't look as frightening as before. It was just a list of dishes in a puffy cover. She would look up something called "grilled vegetables" and say it aloud. How difficult could that be?

Her lover was smiling. "I can't believe you're going to order!" he said.

He was right. It was too late. If she ordered what she wanted now, it would be a confession that for almost a year now she'd been eating food she didn't even like. On the other hand, she felt that she couldn't eat spinach any longer, not a single bite.

Ružena put the menu back.

"We can't see each other anymore," she said.

Her excuse was simple and clear.

"Pavel is coming."

# ROUNDUP OF RECIPES

## 1. Salad Olivier

Salad Olivier is the Russian's Thanksgiving turkey. I can't think of any other holiday dish that would come close to Salad Olivier in popularity. The biggest, most cherished, and most important holiday in Russia is New Year's Eve, and Salad Olivier has always been the centerpiece of that holiday meal. There are so many childhood memories and nostalgic cravings centered around Olivier that it's hard to say what really makes it so important, the dish itself or the complicated emotions that arise with it. There are many stories of its origins and just as many versions of an original recipe, so I don't trust any of them. The core ingredients are boiled potatoes, eggs, pickles, and some kind of chopped meat; the rest is open to interpretation. Here, I'm including two of the traditional class-oriented versions and a third one I created especially for health-conscious Americans, with the vague hope of persuading them that Salad Olivier is well worth eating and can be quite delicious.

PLEBEIAN VERSION

> Bologna from a Russian food store
> Boiled potatoes
> Pickles
> Boiled egg
> Canned peas
> Boiled carrots
> Mayonnaise dressing

*Lots of mayonnaise is essential; add more and more until the salad makes a wet slurping sound while you mix it, similar to the sound of the snow slush on the streets of Manhattan when you step in it. There is not enough mayonnaise until the salad makes that sucking sound.*

*The plebeian version is usually served in a two-gallon enameled bowl. The important thing is to pile up the salad so high that it forms a sloppy mound in the middle of the bowl.*

ARISTOCRATIC VERSION

> Boiled chicken breast
> Boiled potatoes
> Pickles
> Boiled egg
> Canned peas

# Roundup of Recipes

Possibly a peeled green apple
Half mayonnaise/half sour cream dressing
*(the same slurping sound is expected)*

*The aristocratic version—absolutely no car-*
*rots—is served in an elegant cut-crystal bowl.*
*There should be the same mound in the center,*
*but a neatly formed one. The mound is shaped*
*with the back of a mixing spoon and smoothed*
*down along the sides as you would do when icing*
*a cake. Most people also decorate their salads.*
*You will find a really nice outlet for your aristo-*
*cratism and creativity in adorning the salad.*
*There are many elegant ways to lay slices of eggs*
*and/or pickles on top of your salad mound.*

## SOMETHING-AMERICANS-MIGHT-EAT VERSION

Grilled chicken or turkey breast

*(excellent way to use leftover*
*Thanksgiving turkey)*

Boiled potatoes
Pickles (very firm and not too sweet)
Boiled egg (or maybe not)
Canned peas (well, you can skip them too)
Possibly a peeled green apple
Mayonnaise dressing

## Roundup of Recipes

*Use just a* little *mayonnaise, so the salad won't be so damn high in fat content (don't even go near the slurping sound), but not low-fat mayonnaise. If you use low-fat mayonnaise, you might as well throw the whole dish out. It will taste a little dry, yes, but your weight won't go up as dramatically as with the two previous versions. Serving on lettuce leaves will help create the illusion that this is a healthy dish.*

*For all versions, potatoes should be boiled in their skins, then peeled and diced. Everything else should be diced as well into tiny little cubes (¼ inch), although the plebeian version might allow larger and sloppier cubes.*

*The ratio of ingredients is as follows: for every two cups of diced potatoes, use one cup of diced meat, one cup of diced egg, one cup of diced pickles, one cup of peas, half a cup of carrots, and half a cup of apple. Or it could be whatever you want.*

*Oh, writing about this made me so hungry. I have a craving for some Olivier. But I'm at a trailer park in Moscow, Pennsylvania. I don't know why it's called Moscow, for there are no Russians and no Russian delis here. I have hardly any ingredients at hand. We're out of eggs, let alone canned peas or pickles, and my car is in the city in my husband's care, and shopping in rural America without a car is a rough sport. So I'm making myself an extra-simple and*

*extra-plebeian version of Olivier, using what I*
*have in the fridge: two boiled potatoes, three*
*slices of nice bologna, and half a tablespoon of*
*mayonnaise. I know this doesn't sound too appe-*
*tizing, but it is, it is, just trust me!*

## 2. SPINACH

This one is going to be easy. We didn't have
spinach in Russia, except the kind that came in
jars as baby food, so there is no family recipe
for spinach. I tried making some of the spinach
dishes I mention in "Slicing Sautéed Spinach,"
based on recipes I found in cookbooks, but none of
them came out very well. Below is the only
spinach recipe I mastered, but since I learned it
only recently, it didn't make it into the collection
of spinach dishes that my characters eat.

> Baby spinach
> Finely sliced red onion
> Sun-dried tomatoes
> Goat cheese
> Balsamic vinegar
> Extra-virgin olive oil

*Take a pile of baby spinach, put it in a bowl, and*
*add as much of the other ingredients as are*
*needed for desired balance.*

## 3. Meatballs

Since two of the stories have meatballs in them, it was particularly important to find an ultimate meatball recipe. I had never cooked meatballs myself, and I wasn't particularly happy with the family recipe, because it seemed like the main goal of my mother's and grandmother's version was to make the meatballs as dry and hard as rye-bread croutons. "Why waste meat?" I would ask them. "Why not just buy croutons and serve them with pasta or mashed potatoes?"

They didn't answer; perhaps they were perfectly satisfied with crouton meatballs. But I wasn't. Now and then, at some family dinner or at a restaurant, I would happen upon a real meatball—large and juicy and perfect.

Russian meatballs are very different from what Americans call *meatballs*. First of all, they are not shaped like balls; they are shaped like a flattened egg, and they are never buried under spaghetti or smothered in tomato sauce but are usually served hot and crispy with mashed potatoes.

I like Russian meatballs so much that I always thought if I ever wrote a story about two women trying to seduce a man with a certain dish, meatballs would be the dish. But where would I find a perfect recipe? Now I have actually written a story about two women trying to seduce a man with Russian meatballs. Neither of my characters is a professional chef, so I searched among families and family recipes. I managed to collect countless versions, but none of them satisfied me. They were all too complicated, too fussy. Meatballs is a very simple dish. I simply couldn't trust a recipe that required more than twenty ingredients.

And then suddenly found the right one. I knew it was the right one the second I heard it (actually, I read it in a friend's e-mail). Surprisingly, this recipe came not from a seasoned grandma but from a single father who didn't know how to cook and who learned to cook meatballs so he could feed his daughter. This is his recipe:

"Take a pound of regular ground turkey, put it in a bowl, add one egg, some bread soaked in milk (three or four thick slices of white bread, half a cup of milk), lots of garlic and salt and pepper, and mix it. Then pour a little olive oil onto a hot skillet and do this: form the meatball-shaped thing with your hands and throw it onto the skillet, keep the water running, rinse your hands from time to time. [I think it's better to keep a basin of water nearby, so as not to waste water.] Fry meatballs five minutes on each side."

I tried it and it worked. The meatballs came out crispy on the outside, juicy on the inside. The only problem was that they weren't ruinous enough for one's health, and I needed a killer recipe. After some consideration, I simply took my friend's recipe, substituted extravagant red meat for mild ground turkey, and added mind-blowing amounts of fat. Actually, the character in "Luda and Milena" dies after eating these meatballs, but not as a *result* of eating them. I can't guarantee that meatballs based on the recipe I used in the story can actually kill a person. The recipe has never been properly tested to determine that. However, it contains such an extravagant quantity of red meat and fat, most doctors I know swear that consistent consumption of this dish will cause if not immediate death than eventual clogging of the arteries. So if you need to kill yourself or another person and don't mind that the process will be slow and painful, here is the recipe.

½ pound fat ground lamb
½ pound fat ground beef
1 cup white bread soaked in heavy cream
1 finely grated medium onion
2 or 3 finely chopped garlic cloves
1 egg
¼ pound butter, lard, bacon, or any other
    spectacular animal-fat product to use
    for frying

## 4. Cold Borscht

I'm sitting on the deck, leaning against the wall of the trailer we rent in Moscow, Pennsylvania. My kids are splashing in the lake, and I feel so jealous. It's 88 degrees Fahrenheit outside, and about 130 inside. Plus there's the smell of fried lard and garlic. I've just cooked several batches of meatballs to make sure I got the recipe right. I did get it right, by the way—it's a killer recipe. You can easily have a heart attack simply by cooking those meatballs; you don't even have to eat them.

The last thing I want to do right now is to think about borscht.

The characters in my story are eating rich, hot borscht, which is a wonderful dish when there is a February snowstorm outside, or at least a chilly November rain. But right now, what I really want to eat is cold borscht. It is probably my favorite summer food, being that rare combination of very healthy, cheap, extremely easy to make, and amazingly delicious. Here is the recipe.

> One 24 oz. jar of borscht from the Jewish
> section of a supermarket (in Moscow,
> Pennsylvania, it's right next to the
> Mexican and Italian foods)
> 3 hard-boiled eggs (or just egg whites)

1 medium seedless cucumber, or three
    or four kirbys, peeled
1 scallion
Half a bunch of fresh dill (or a pinch
    of dry dill)
Sour cream
Lemon slices
Dijon mustard (optional)

*What you do is this: Let the jar of borscht chill in the fridge for at least an hour before opening it. The soup is best when it is very cold. Finely chop the eggs, cucumber (chopped cucumber smells amazing!), scallions, and dill, put them in a bowl, add a pinch of salt, and let them stay in the fridge for half an hour, so they can both chill and adjust to one another's company. Then divide them between four bowls (this recipe should yield four portions, although I could easily eat it all alone), and pour the borscht over, shaking the jar before pouring, to lift the beet slices off the bottom. Sometimes I add a teaspoon of Dijon mustard; I mix it with a little borscht liquid, pour it back in the jar, and shake it well.*

*    Serve with sour cream and slices of lemon; I like to squeeze my lemon slice with a spoon to add a tangy taste to the soup.*

## 5. Hot Borscht

Today, it's a different picture. It's been raining nonstop, and it's suddenly cold outside. I'm wearing jeans and a sweater and my husband's thick socks—I can't believe I was sweating in a tank top and shorts just a few days ago. The gas heater in our trailer has been broken for years, and the owners won't bother fixing it. They never live here themselves, and summer renters apparently don't need heat. "It's a rundown trailer," my husband says. "What do you expect?" We rent it for seven weeks for the price of what you'd typically pay for two, and I'm usually happy with the bargain. Not on a day like today, though. We tried an electric heater, but it was expensive and seemed to warm only the ten-inch area around it. What we do is this: We turn all four stove burners on and put four large pots of water on to boil. (We could try baking pies, but there are mice living in the oven, and I really don't want to go there.) While the water is boiling on the stove, we cuddle with the kids under a huge blanket that the neighbors lent us and watch *Young Frankenstein* on my computer. (We never get tired of watching *Young Frankenstein*.) Well, I think, since we need to keep four large pots on the stove, why not cook borscht in one of them? I can cook and still keep an eye on *Young Frankenstein*.

3 or 4 fresh beets
3 or 4 potatoes
1 medium carrot
1 medium onion
3 stalks of celery
Olive oil
2 tablespoons tomato sauce
2 quarts beef broth
Salt and pepper
1 or 2 bay leaves
1 tablespoon white vinegar
Sour cream
Chopped parsley and garlic (optional)

*Chop vegetables and sauté them right in the soup pot, in a little olive oil and the tomato sauce, for 15 to 20 minutes. Pour the store-brought beef broth over the mixture. When it starts to boil, add salt, pepper, a bay leaf or two, and vinegar, and let the soup simmer until everything is tender, which sometimes takes so long that* Young Frankenstein *ends before my borscht is ready.*

*Hot borscht is served with sour cream just like cold borscht. I like to chop some parsley and garlic, smash the two together with a pinch of salt, and sprinkle this over a little island of sour cream in the bowls.*

*For some reason, it always seems warmer in*

*the trailer when you make borscht than when you simply boil water. And there is another advantage. We don't have enough space at the table, so we eat balancing our hot bowls in our laps. And the laps get warm too.*

*Too bad my son won't eat borscht; he won't eat any cooked vegetable. But he will eat some vegetables raw, which brings me to the broccoli recipe.*

## 6. BROCCOLI

I haven't found a way to make cooked broccoli delicious, so we mostly eat it raw. Every Monday, we go to the farmers' market in Scranton to buy some. The trip itself is an adventure: first up and down on hilly Route 307, then into the maze of Scranton's streets, where run-down wooden buildings alternate with Gothic churches and Masonic temples. Once we make it to the market, the kids get a dollar each to stuff themselves with cider, doughnuts, and cookies (Scranton's market is so cheap you can really gorge on a dollar), and I don't feel guilty because I'm buying a lot of vegetables. The broccoli is wonderful there. The bunches are a bright, sunny shade of green, they are firm but tender, and they taste fresh but not too grassy. My son's favorite part (and mine too) is the stalk. I just cut it off, removing the tough part on the very bottom, and peel the rest with a potato peeler. My daughter loves florets, but only with a dip, which we make like this:

> 1 cup low-fat plain yogurt
> 1 clove of garlic (finely chopped)
> Chopped parley
> Lemon juice
> Salt to taste

Look, both kids are eating broccoli! How I love them!

—L.V.